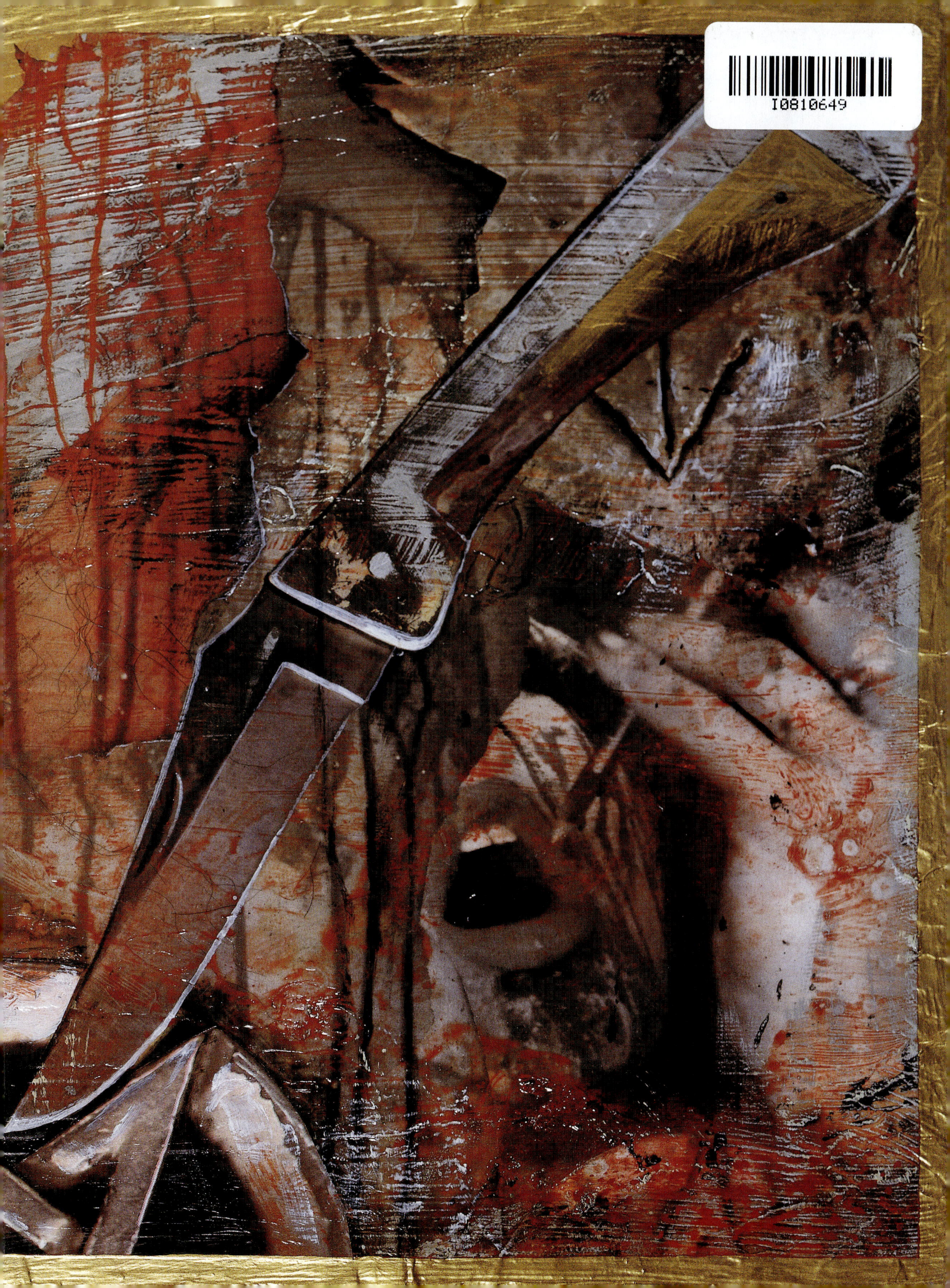

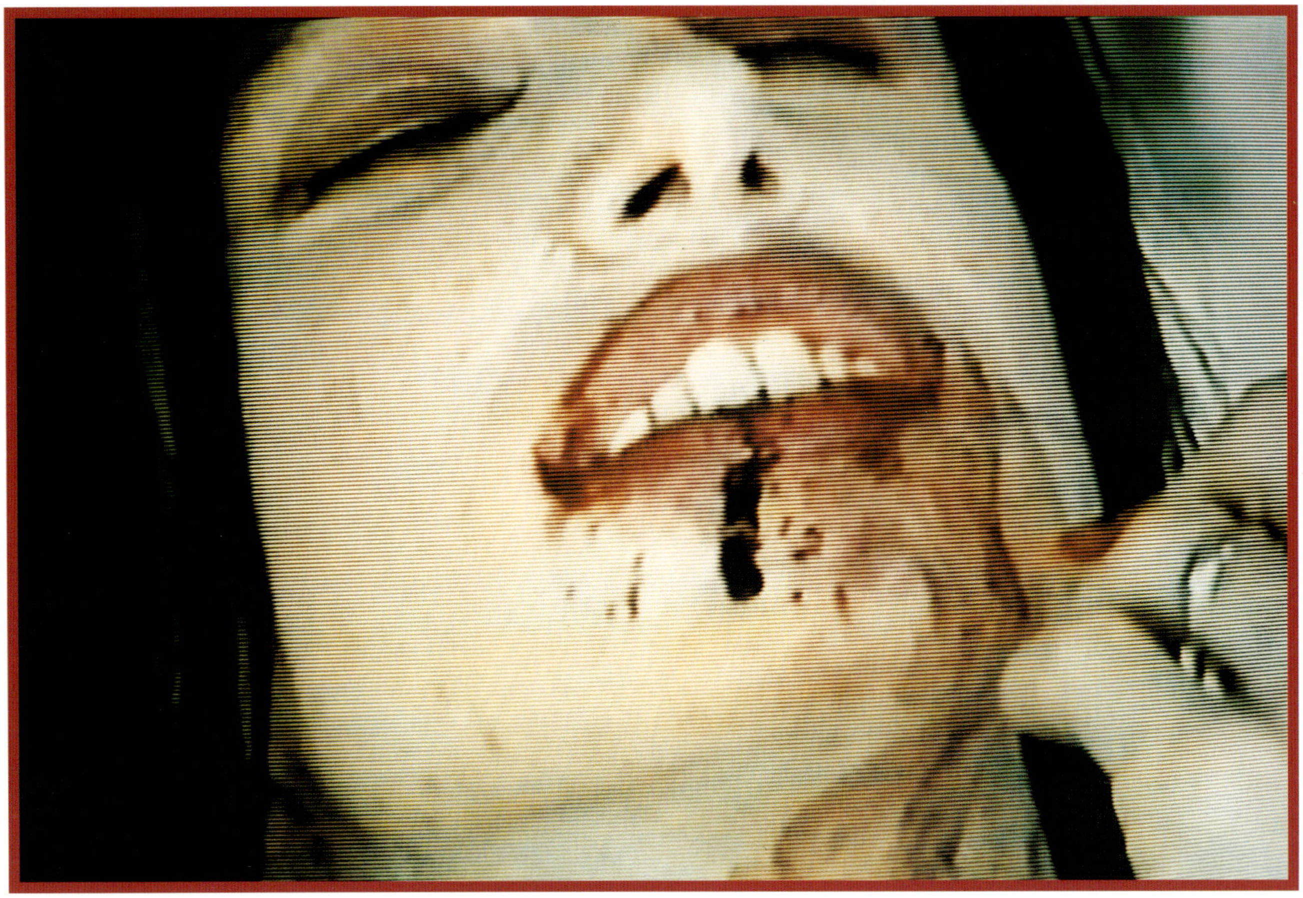

Published by Last Gasp Books, 777 Florida St., San Francisco, CA 94110 USA
http://www.lastgasp.com

Book design and layout by David Aaron Clark and Charles Pinion.

Other Charles Gatewood titles and videos are available through Last Gasp.

Special Thanks: Alan McNaughton, Mistress Shane, Baba Ron, Mistress Sarah, the Aesthetic Meat Foundation, Mistress Kate, M 5tevens, Mistress Midori, Reverend Steven Johnson Leyba and the U.S.A.F. at http://www.slip.net/~void/usaf.html; Dana Smith, Jim Morton, Catharine Clark Gallery, San Francisco.

Endpaper collage by Steven Johnson Leyba.

This book depicts unusual body practices and is to be sold to and viewed by adults only.

ISBN 0-86719-443-X (softcover)
ISBN 0-86719-447-2 (hardcover)

TRUE BLOOD

Photographs by
CHARLES GATEWOOD

Text by
DAVID AARON CLARK

Sun In Scorpio
1997

LAST GASP BOOKS SAN FRANCISCO

the village is
hemmed in on all
sides by the forest
in winter the snow
is trampled
red and dull brown
look up from your fire
at night and there
will be half a dozen
white faces pressed
against the windowpane
in summer we nail the
hearts of vampires dripping
rosary beads and skin pouches
full of sharp teeth to
doors and treetrunks,
scrawl LEECHES BEWARE in
blood and garlic pulp
when I was a child
my sister pinned me
to the floor, sucking at
the flesh of my arm until
Father pulled off me
saying it's nothing
to play at, leading us
out to the barn where
the sow and her litter
were lying in the straw
with their throats
ripped out
we were beaten and
sent to bed without
supper and sat up
ventured too far
beyond the birch thickets
and returned home
three days later smeared
with blood and clay demanding
that Mother draw her a bath
her eyes were as
yellow as gallowswort
and Father drove her away
with an axe
for about a month afterward
we would hear her crying
out by the woodpile
Father set traps for her
but she was too clever
once I left her some flowers
tied up with a blue ribbon
and in the morning there was a
smooth white finger bone
in its place which I
sewed up inside my pillow.

—Danielle Willis

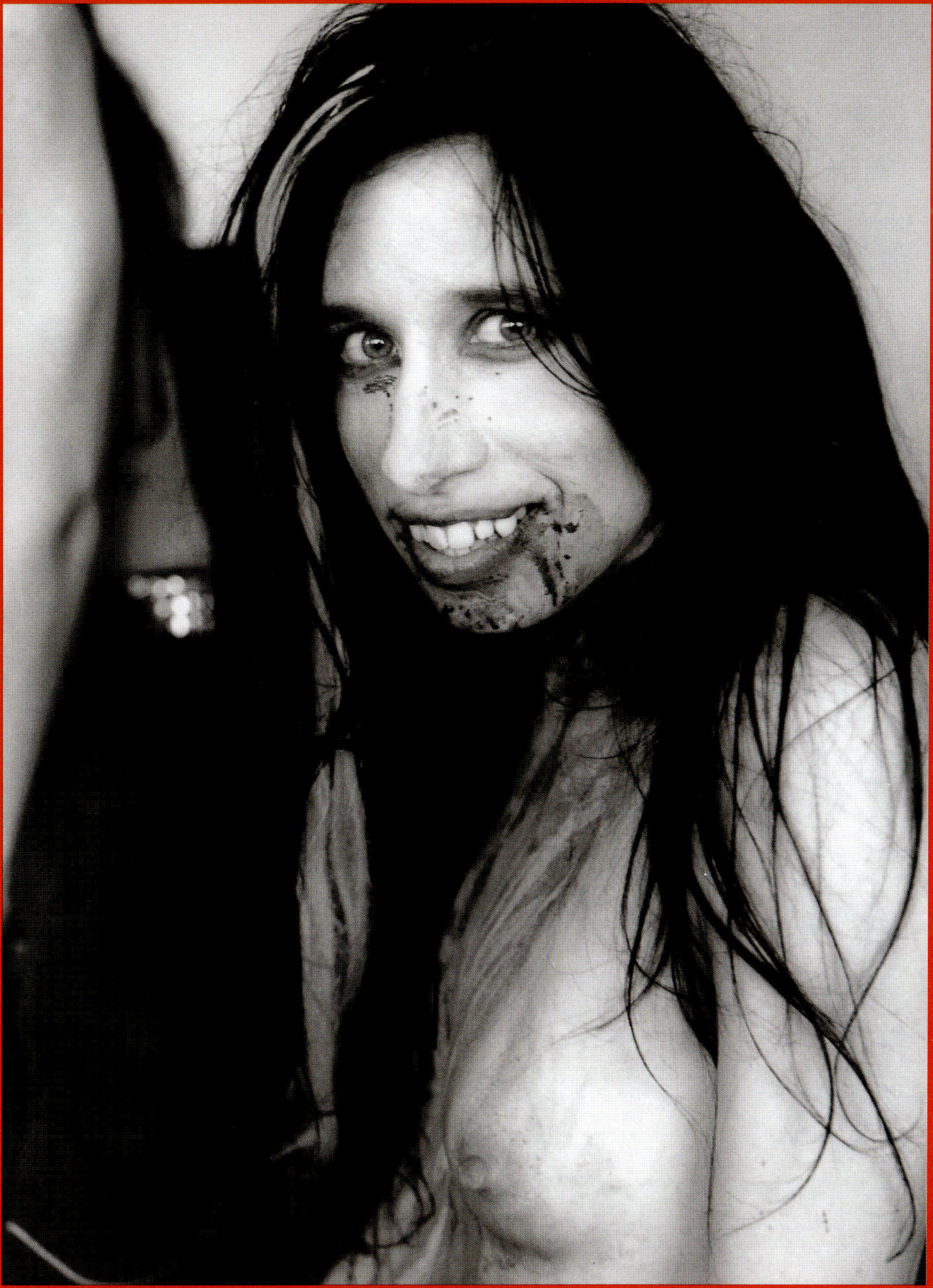

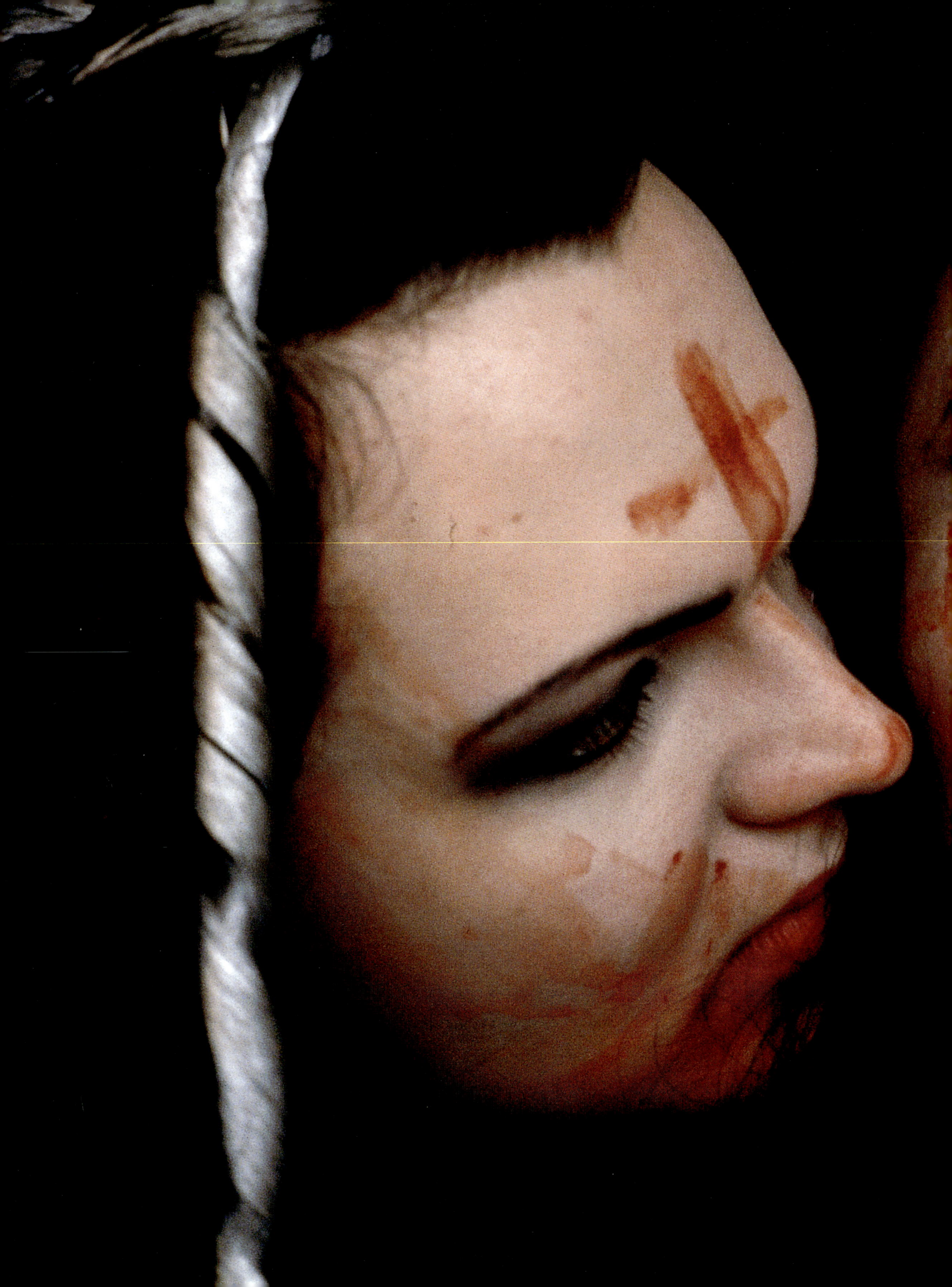

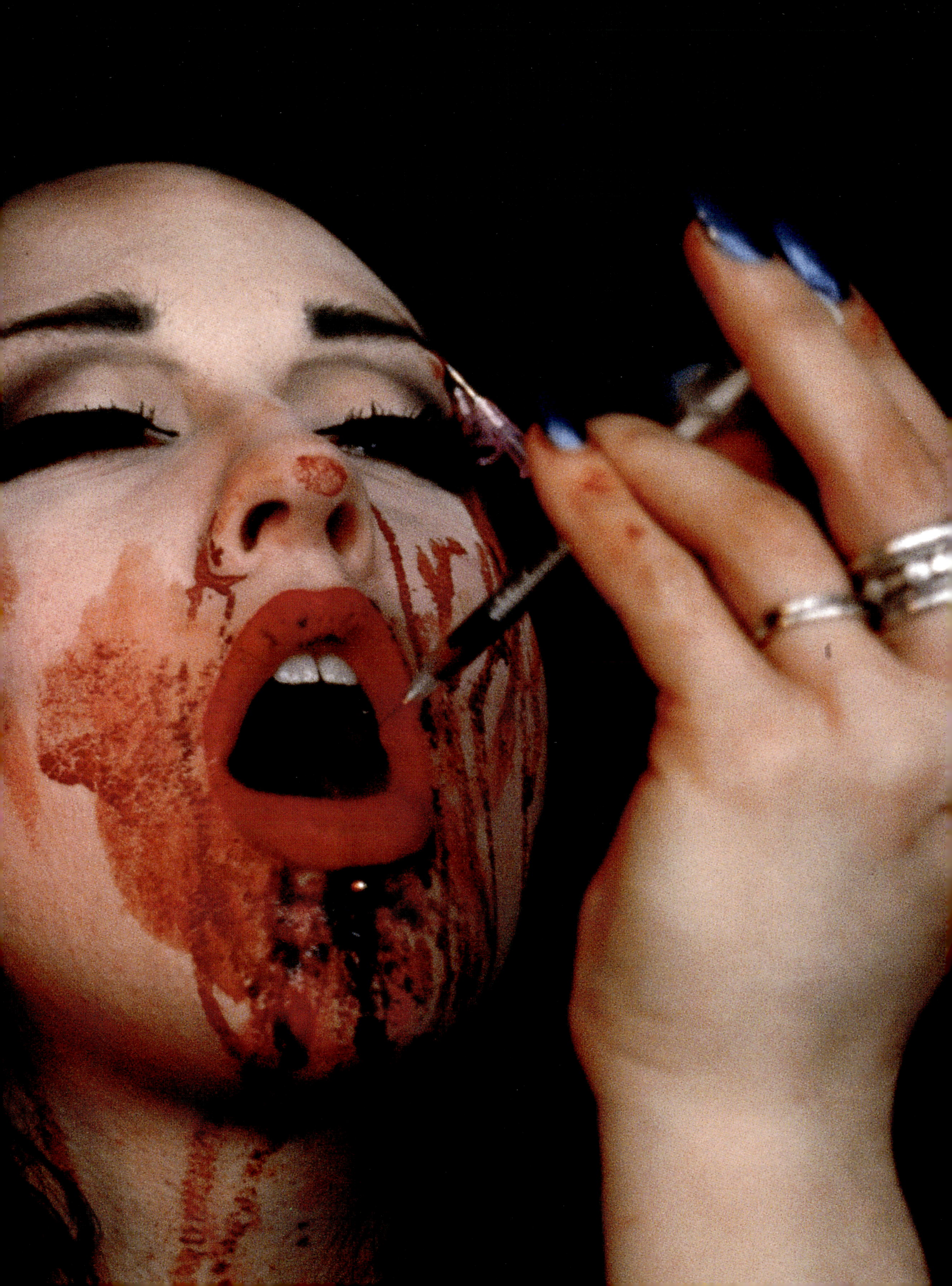

All hail the vermillion We; our mingling is absolute. Twin faces of hunger, silver in our beauty. Vampires of the sacred heart, hosting a blood orgy of the damned.

Curse the stuff, already cooling, already clogging, but still precious drug that injects the most crimson high of all: Life itself, in all its coagulated black glory. Heaven ever after, in the speed shivers of evaporating hallucination.

You are the Girl With The Black Hole Eyes and I am your stillborn sister. We suck the same hypodermic teat, recycling the desperation in our souls. Drawing forth the sugar that sizzles in a bow of explosions across your cheek, that we draw the signs of sacrifice in with vibrating finger.

I follow the tributary up your arm with suddenly dry tongue, provoked and wanting, but knowing how easy it is to suck that little hole of yours sere. And then I'd never be able to drink again. Don't tremble; I like to think of you as made of marble, a work of human art that defeats nature even as it celebrates it. And now that cold stone weeps warmly, a dark miracle promulgating a sticky new faith.

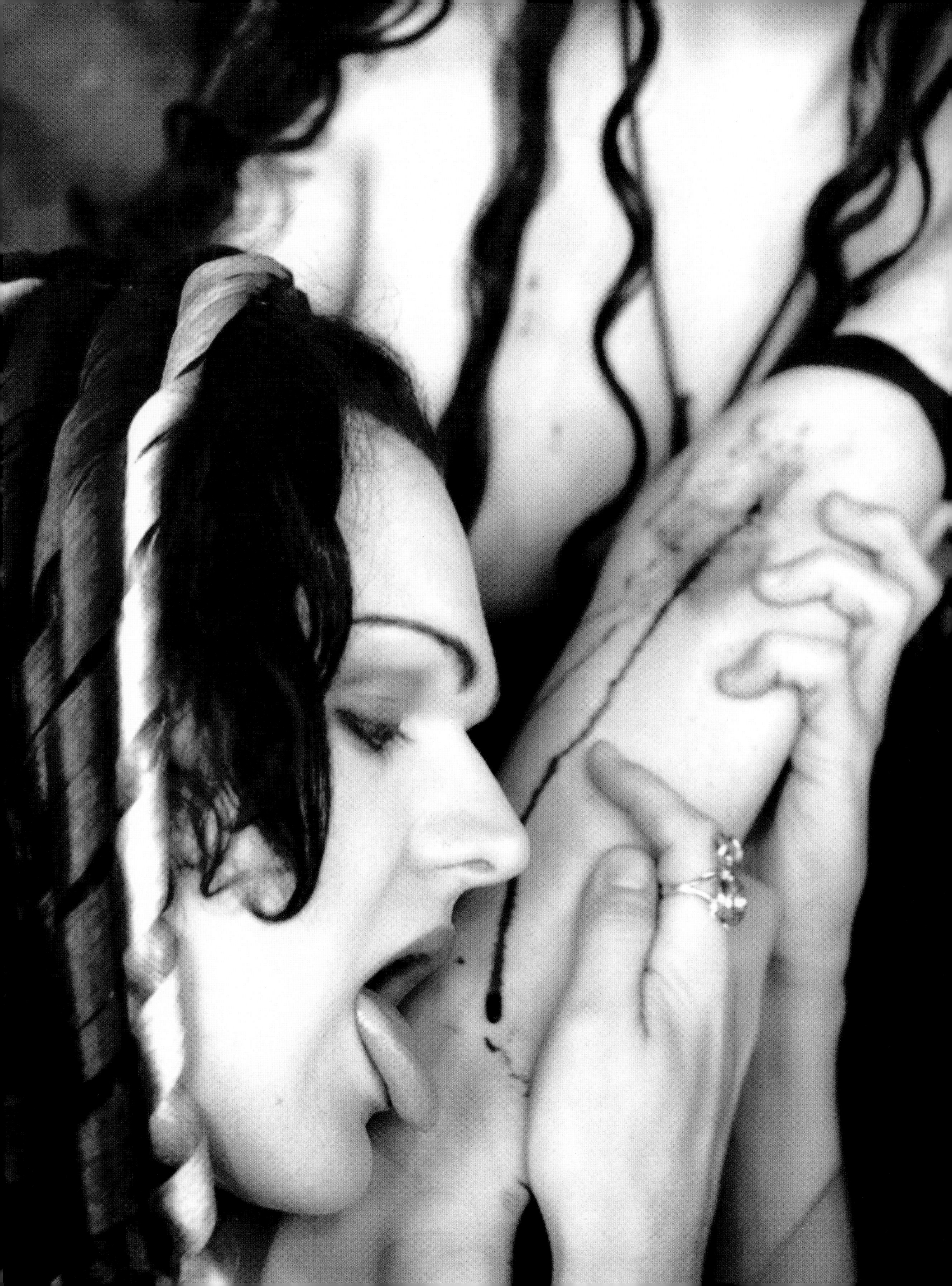

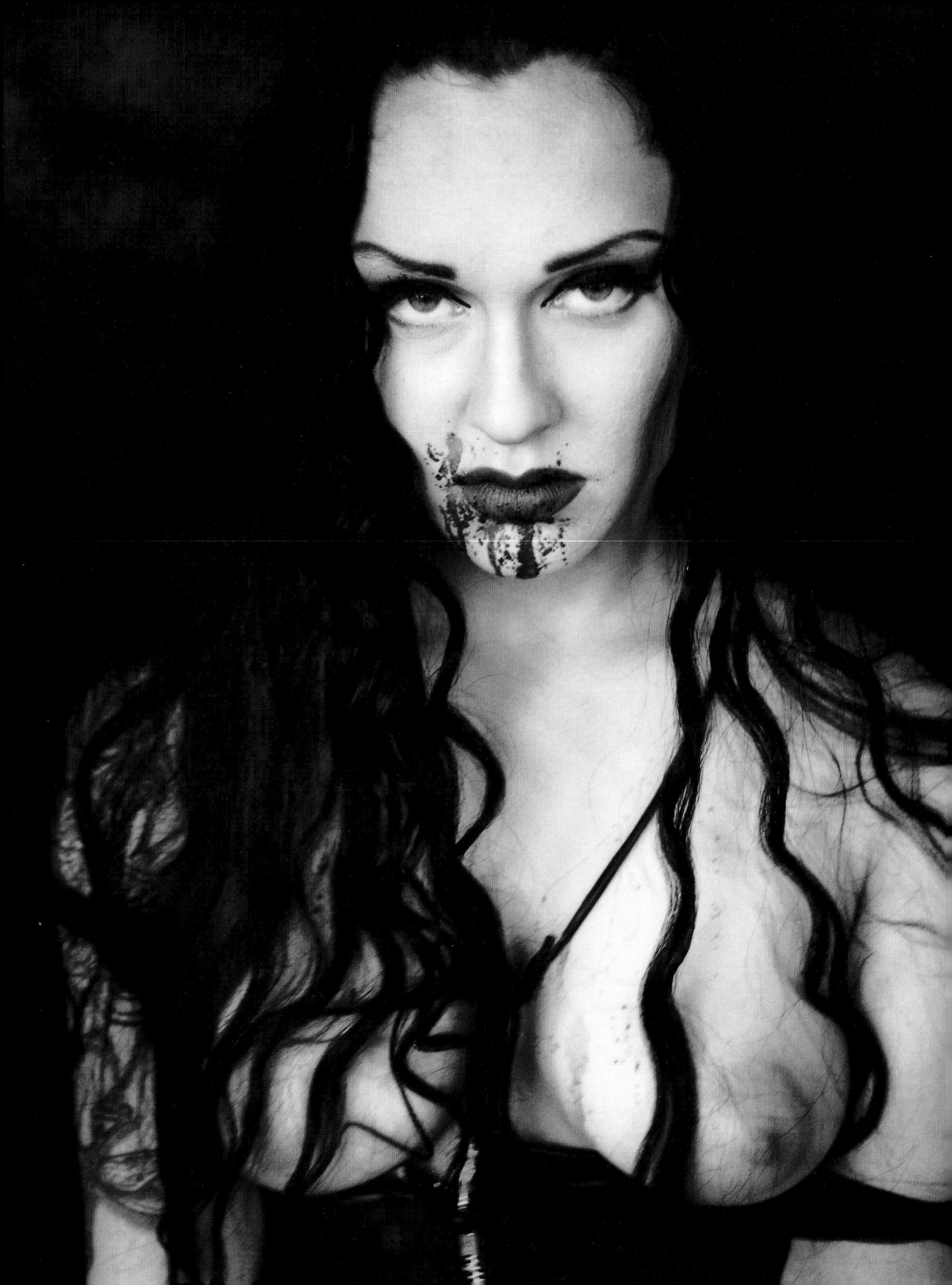

In your smug pout I see every daughter of Lilith, that demon's concubine whose barren womb can never be christened, and in whose honor have been built an endless string of cold temples full of hungry idols to which men of every race have been all too anxious to offer oblation. Bored by your mocking death rituals even before they're complete, you are a changeling weaned on fairy tales in which everyone comes to bad ends, and only the monster is beautiful.

So yes, you are beautiful. You are a fairy tale. You are eternal, if only in men's gazes. And I know you by at least 17 of your names, demon of Friday:

Lilith
Odam
Abeko
Kea
Satrina
Talto
Kali
Partasah
Abito
Batna
Patrota
Podo
Amizo
Eilo
Ita
Izorpo
Kokos

But I am not afraid, for by your cruel gleaming example you have awoken and provoked the anti-divine in me as well: the demiurge towards a career of immolations. I shall be Leliel, prince of conception, soldier for Abraham against the tyrants. An angel happily damned by your side.

We shall drink of ourselves until the end of time.

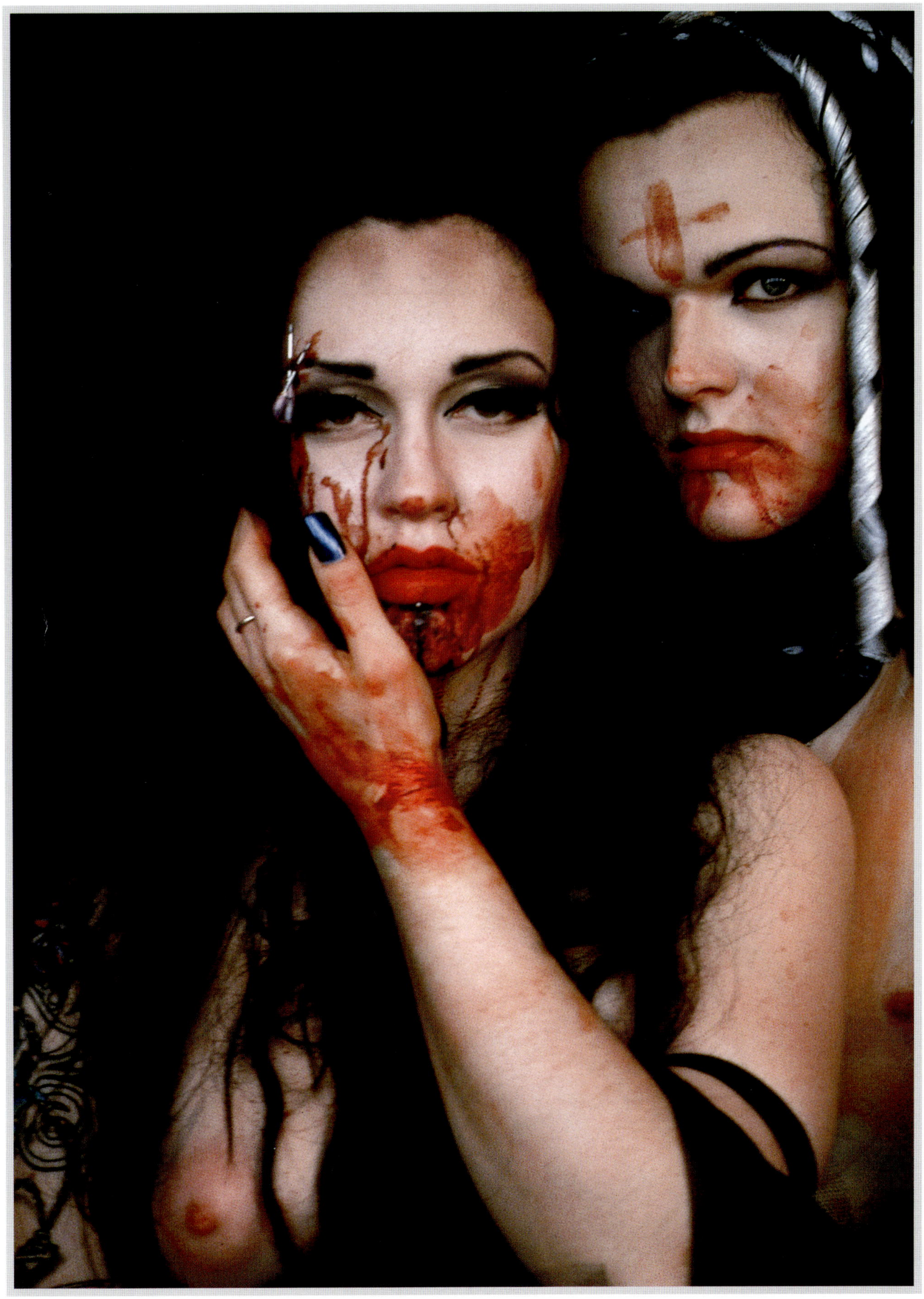

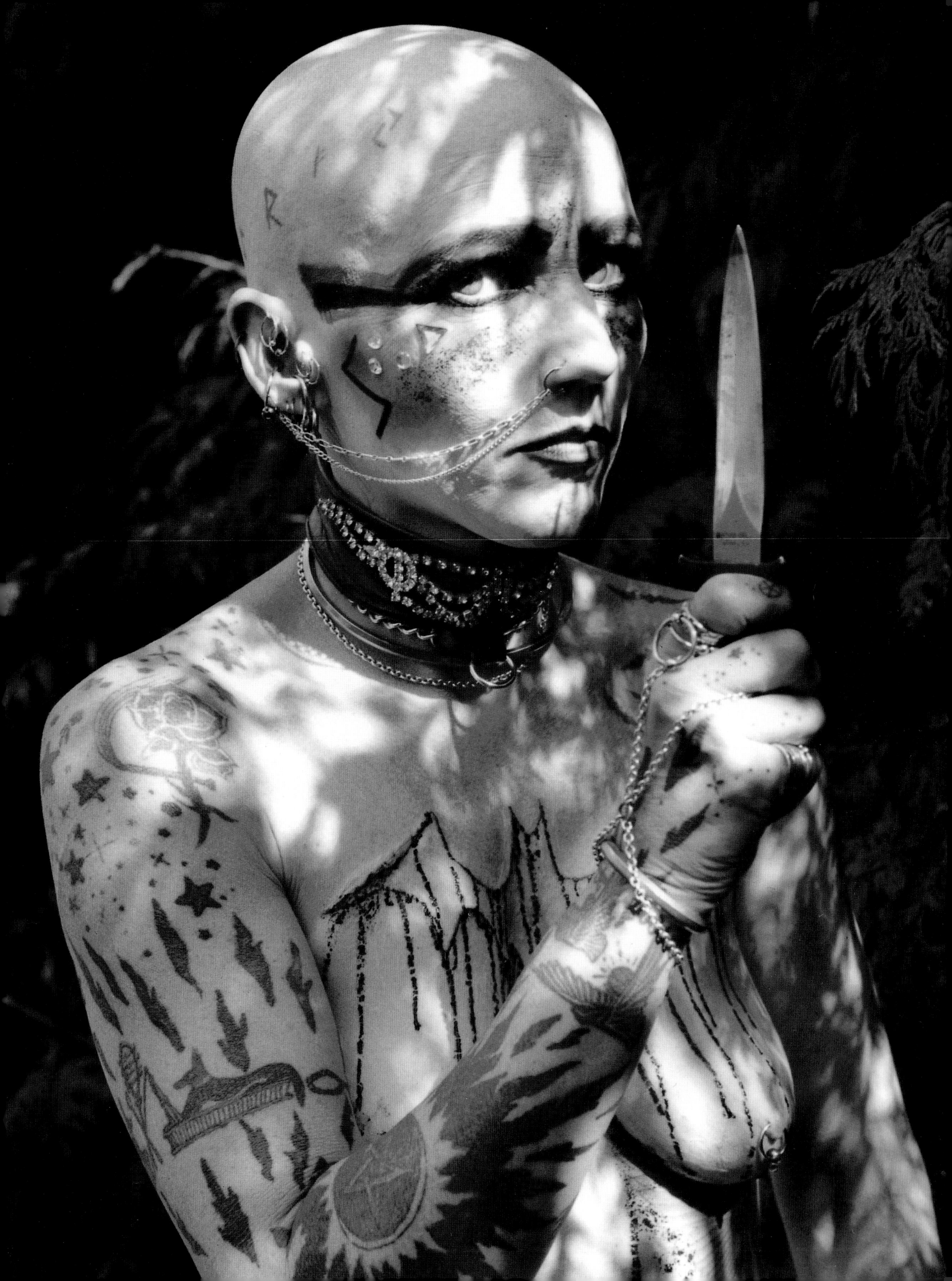

She taunts sanity from the other side.

A bat made of red jewels falls like lace across the crone's chest. An offering to the green world; food for Gaia. It works. Wood Goddess ruffles her bark like scales on an ancient dragon. Trembling under the whispering encouragements of Sister Wind, extends her branch, sap weeping from the green leaf that dangles from the pliable shoot at the furthermost tip of his reach.

Is it steel or iron you've brought into our wedding bed, She asks the painted bride naked at her base.

Iron, from the earth, beaten into a blade more sharp and precise than Fire... iron, with which I shall make you my mistress, the keeper of my rent maidenhead, soaking there into the earth at your roots so it might replenish our vows.

Now crone-slave moves in spastic jig, nerves invaded by her lover's fingers, one each of air earth fire water fifth dimension, massaging the way for that molten finger disengorging from the constantly exploding heart of lava. As crone is penetrated she croons to the wolves and birds to rest their hunger in the fullness of the night, the sun's rays have been forgotten like the day before yesterday's meal.

Her blood is the wine she shares so they might all speak at the same pitch, and burn with understood language.

Her blood is the bridge between her and the oceans.

Her blood is the gift to the sand in the deserts.

Her blood is the lubrication for massive, hidden tectonic gears. Oil for the coming age of Ragnarok.

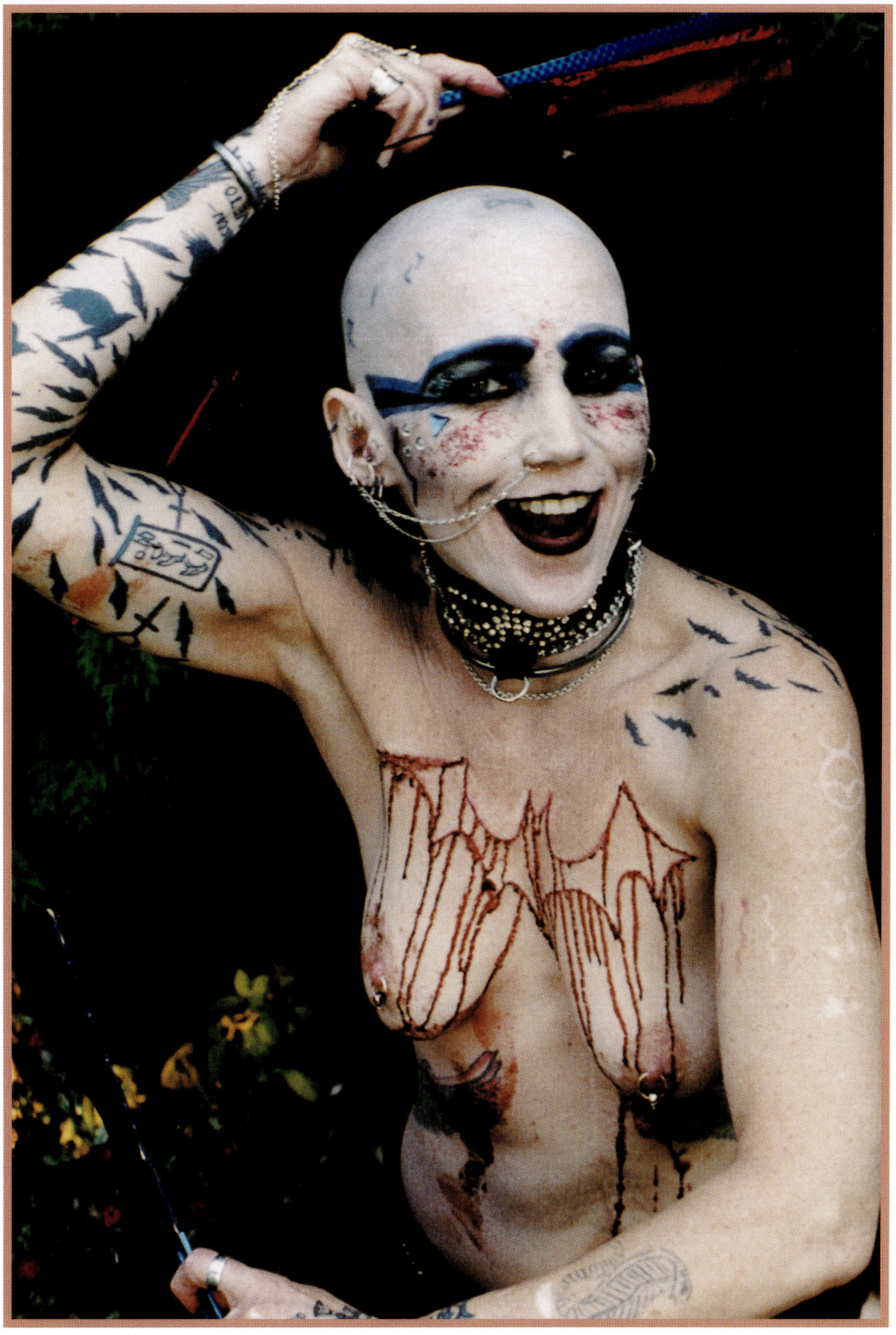

I wear the crown of the bleeding fool; my thoughts directed in a pure, straight path by the implacable trajectory of surgical steel. In this ring of stalwart pain I confront and vanquish all enemy weakness and regret. Possessed by the monkey king, I caper between planet and plane. My passion is for a vision of perpetual fuck between every consciousness. A daisy chain to hell and back, drawing tight around the throat of eternity.

I am evolved towards a day not yet come; I herald its peaceful chaos. I suffer the gray world that precedes its birth, and do not fear its passing.

I am mighty and safe behind these steel bars, infused by the field generated across their gleam. These are the fingers of the blind; they whisper to us in sensual dream language the true landscape of the flesh continuum. Through their sieve is the purity of carnal devotion separated from the vicissitudes of spiritual whim.

I am the sum of my holes. Thanks to them, I am lighter than air. Thanks to them, I can see across a spectrum infused with more rapid vibration: The best view this side of my mother's cunt from the inside out as I took the backwards roller coaster slide into the bright, cold cavern where I first learned to cry.

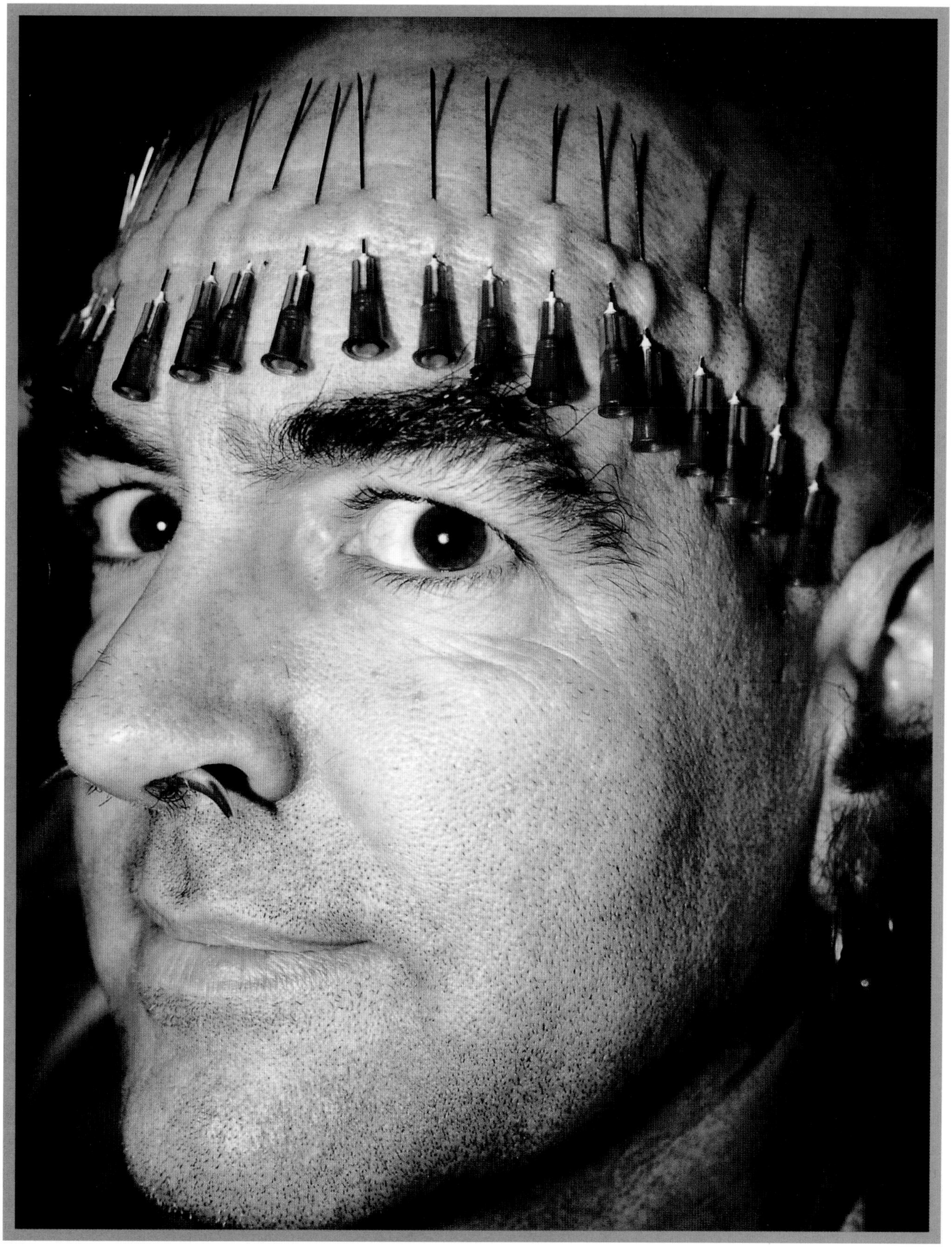

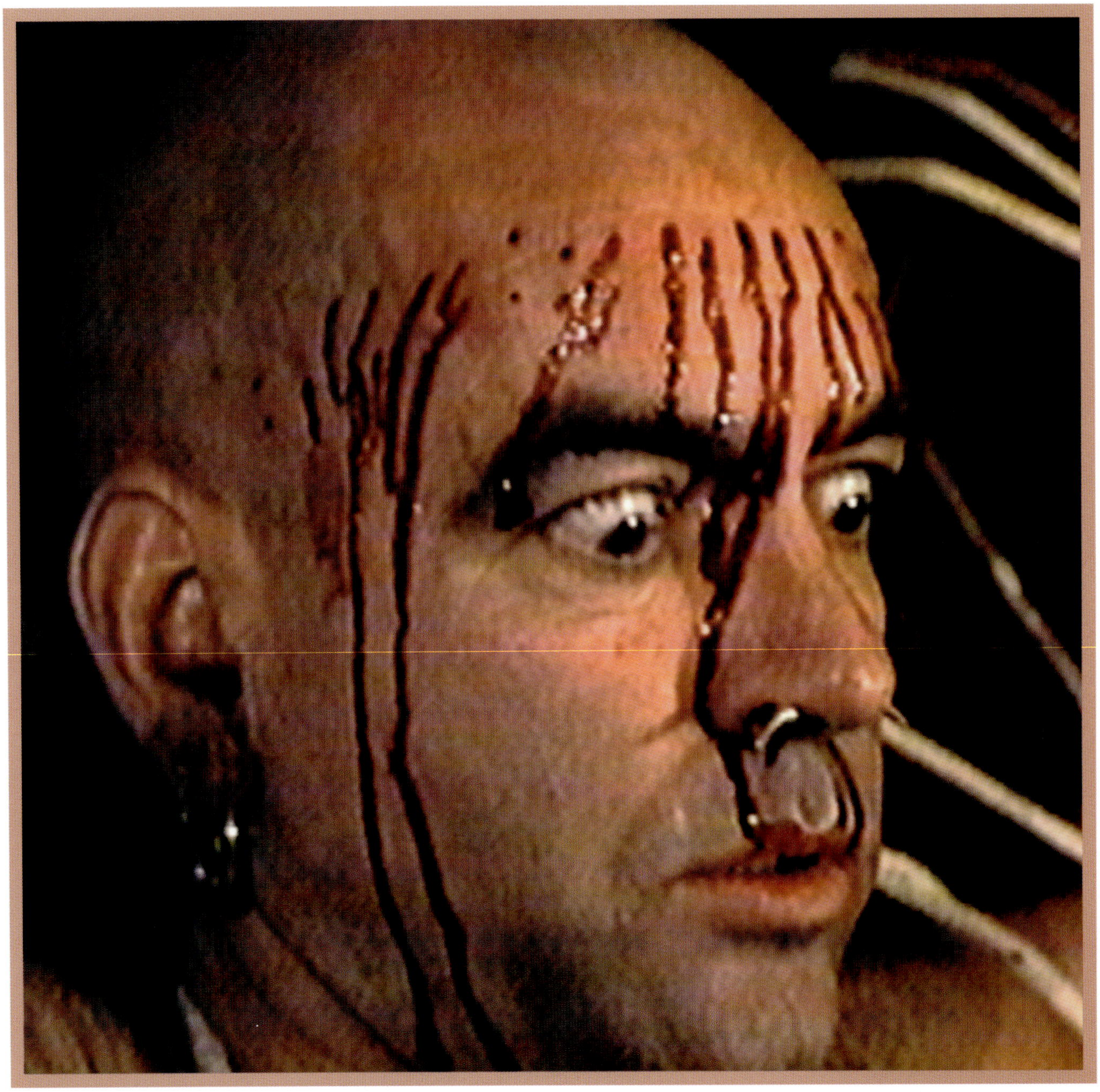

I will walk with the angels through the streets of Orange County. I shall fall to my hands and knees and crawl like a coyote on his belly through the mud, keening with the hungry wail of predestination.

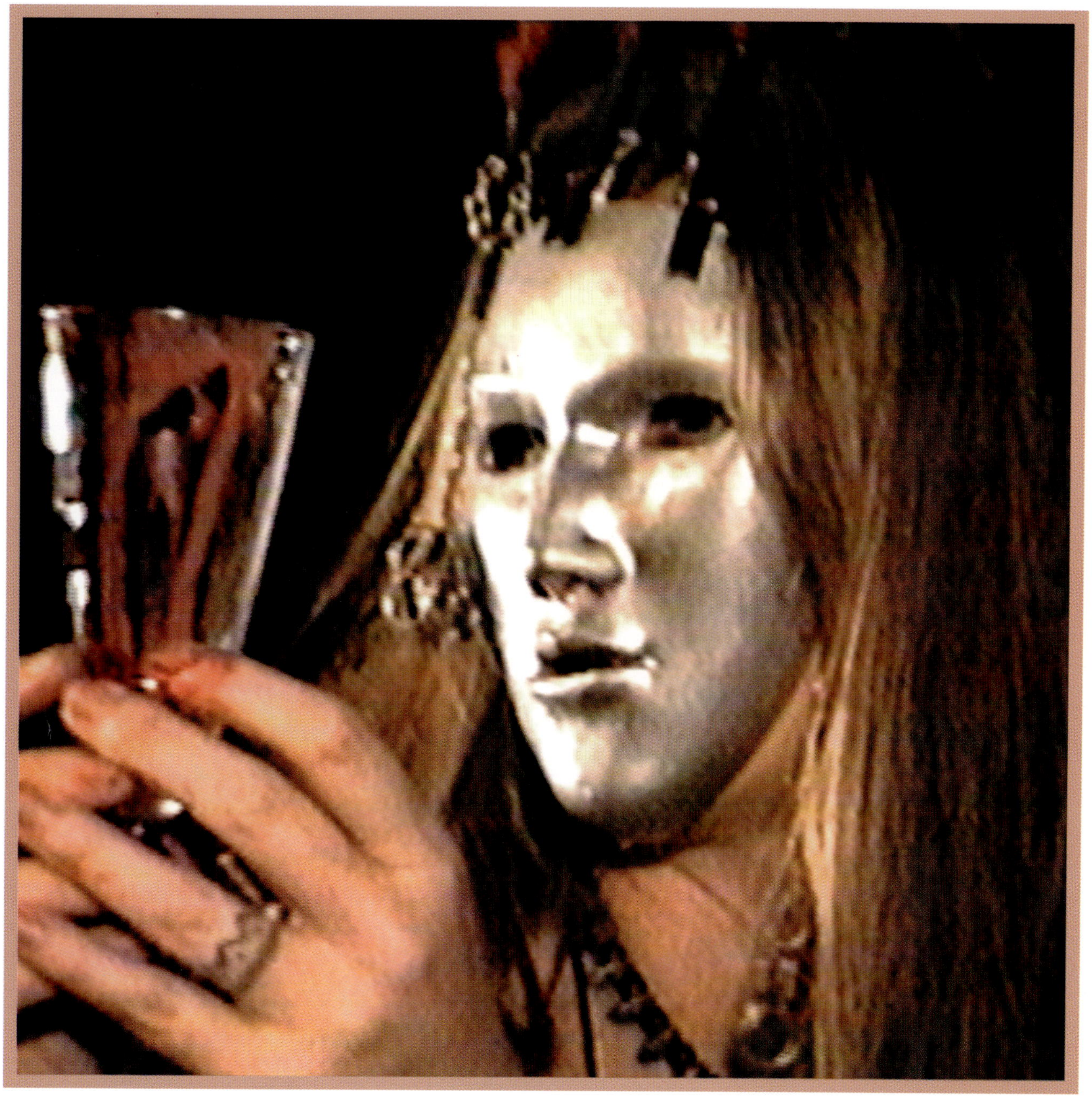

In front of the town fathers my lover will bind me to two rough planks of wood and mortify my flesh, coax forth fluids of many colors into her goblet, of which we will then share.

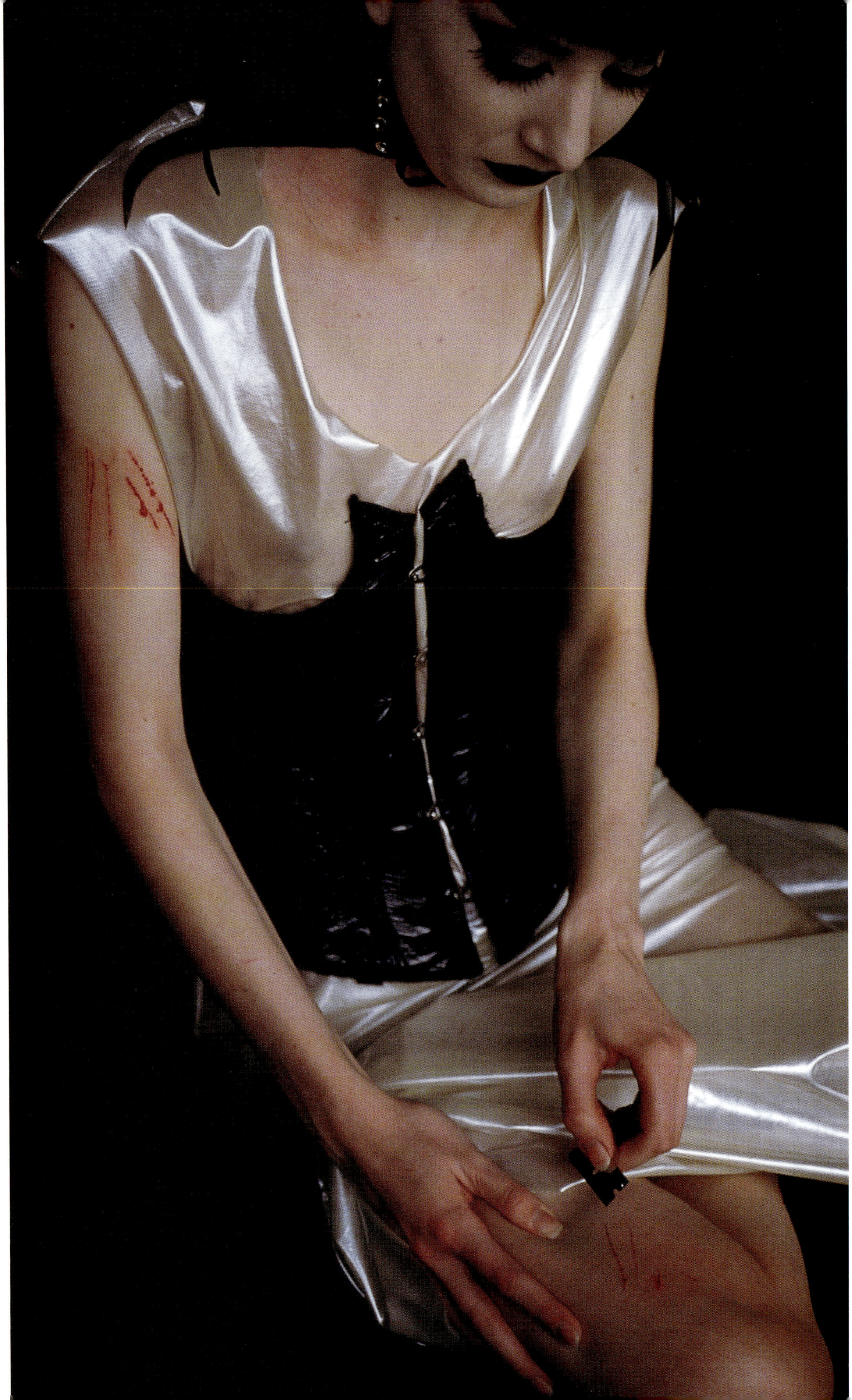

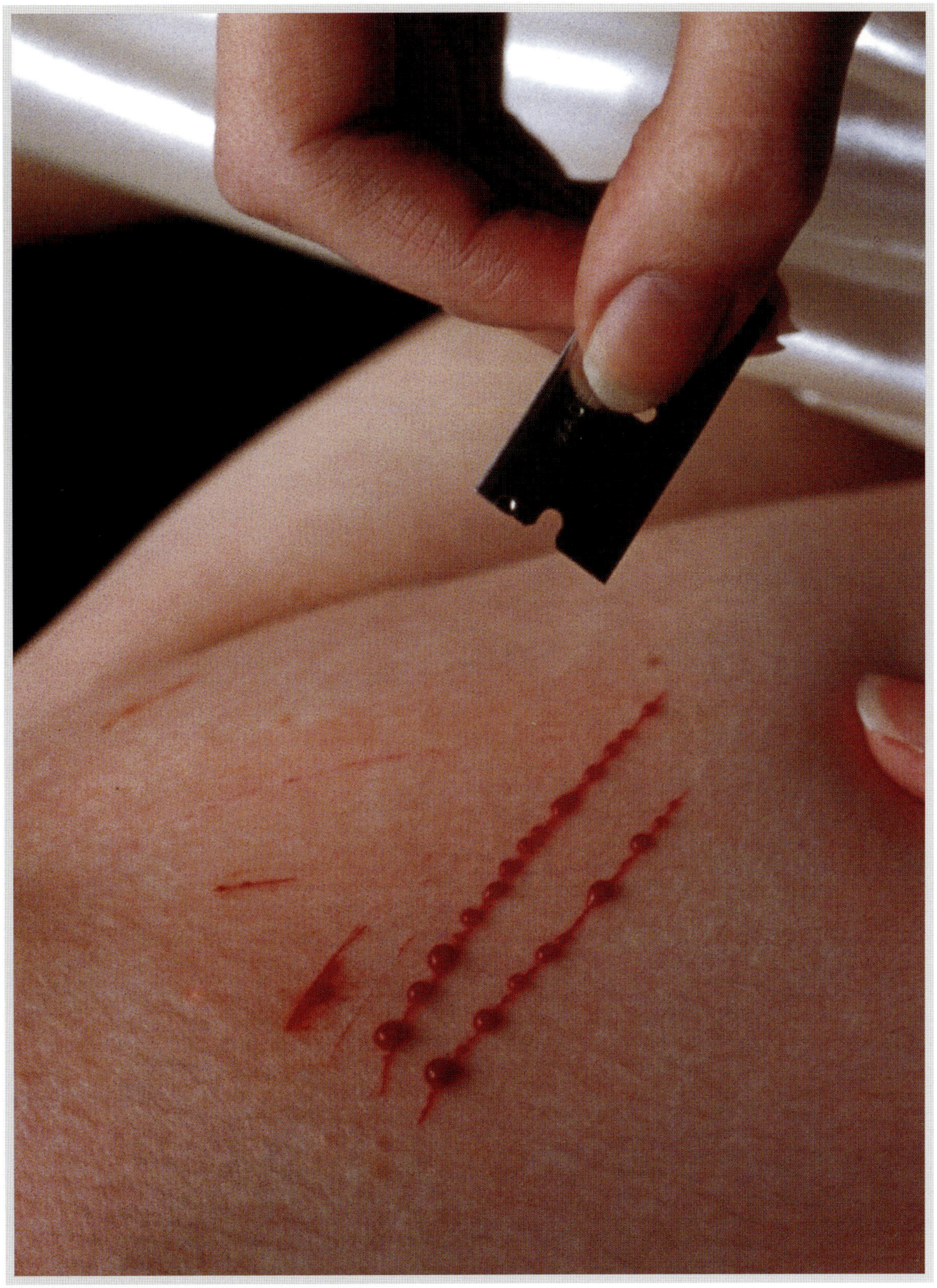

An unknown alphabet suggests itself with each new string of crimson beads. Her own personal language. Come to save her.

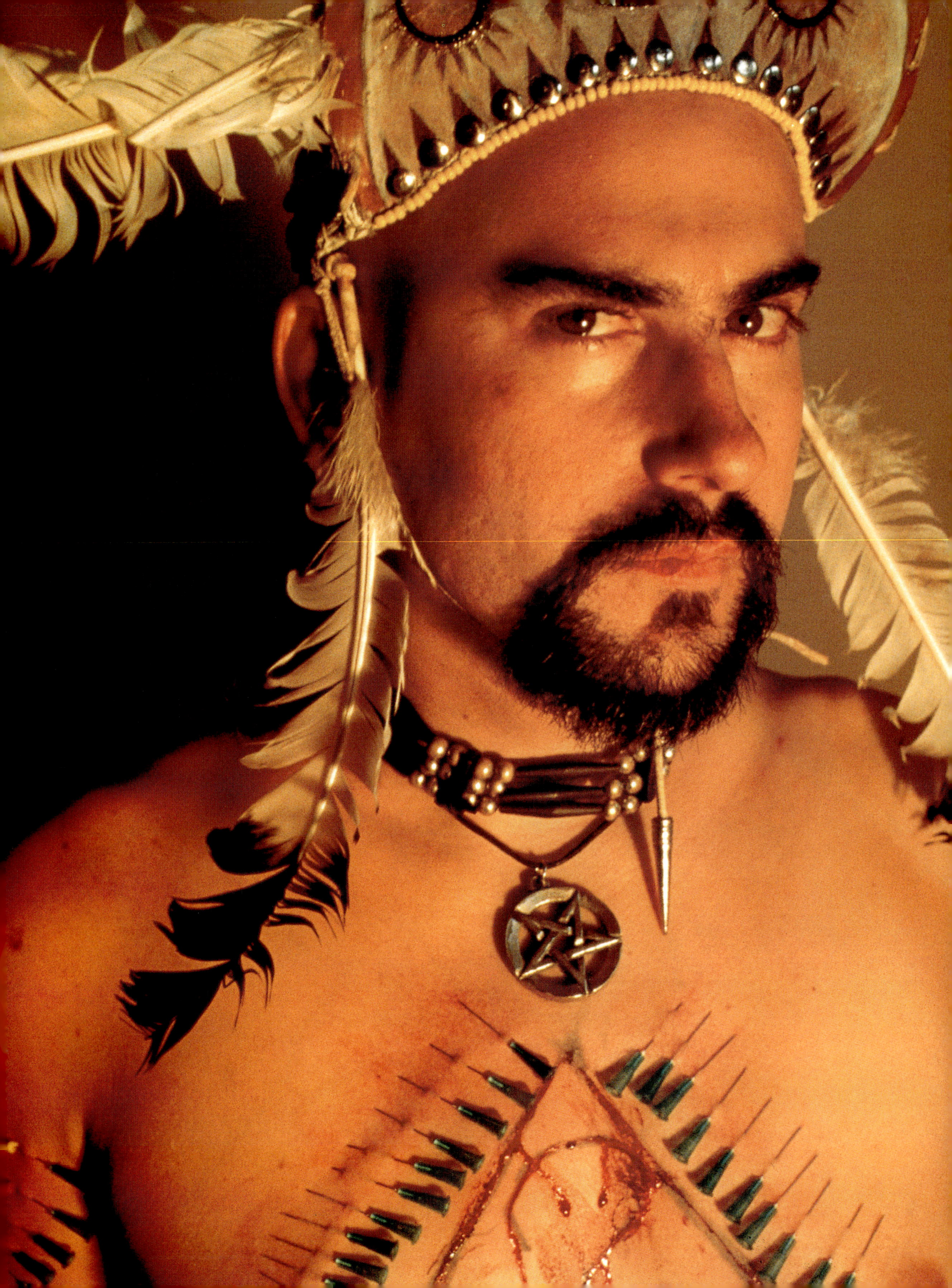

Crazy Indian. Half-breed Apache taking Jack Daniels enemas out in the desert, on his knees before a napalm pentagram. Using his shit and blood to water the blasted playa, stark uncaring beauty, symbol of what one half of him stole from the other. How to battle, then, but to spill your own blood?

Blood gives him prophecy. He soaks his canvas, and begins to paint. Gives his flesh to a tribe of wild knife-wielding squaws who count erotic coup with each slash and burn. He coaxes them with shy skin that yields like butter. They laugh in disbelief and take their pleasure.

As a result, his visions are all orifice and limb, disembodied, sutured, radiant; the creation of a new order through angry geometry, a throb to discover new lands to invade, fresh hearts to rend. besides his own. To cure Crazy Horse of his madness. To restore the hymen of Pocahontas. To win Tonto his own mini-series.

For that he would sell his soul to Satan. And does. The contract is framed on his wall, next to tomahawk and dildo. Visitors to his studio are afraid to ask if it's a joke.

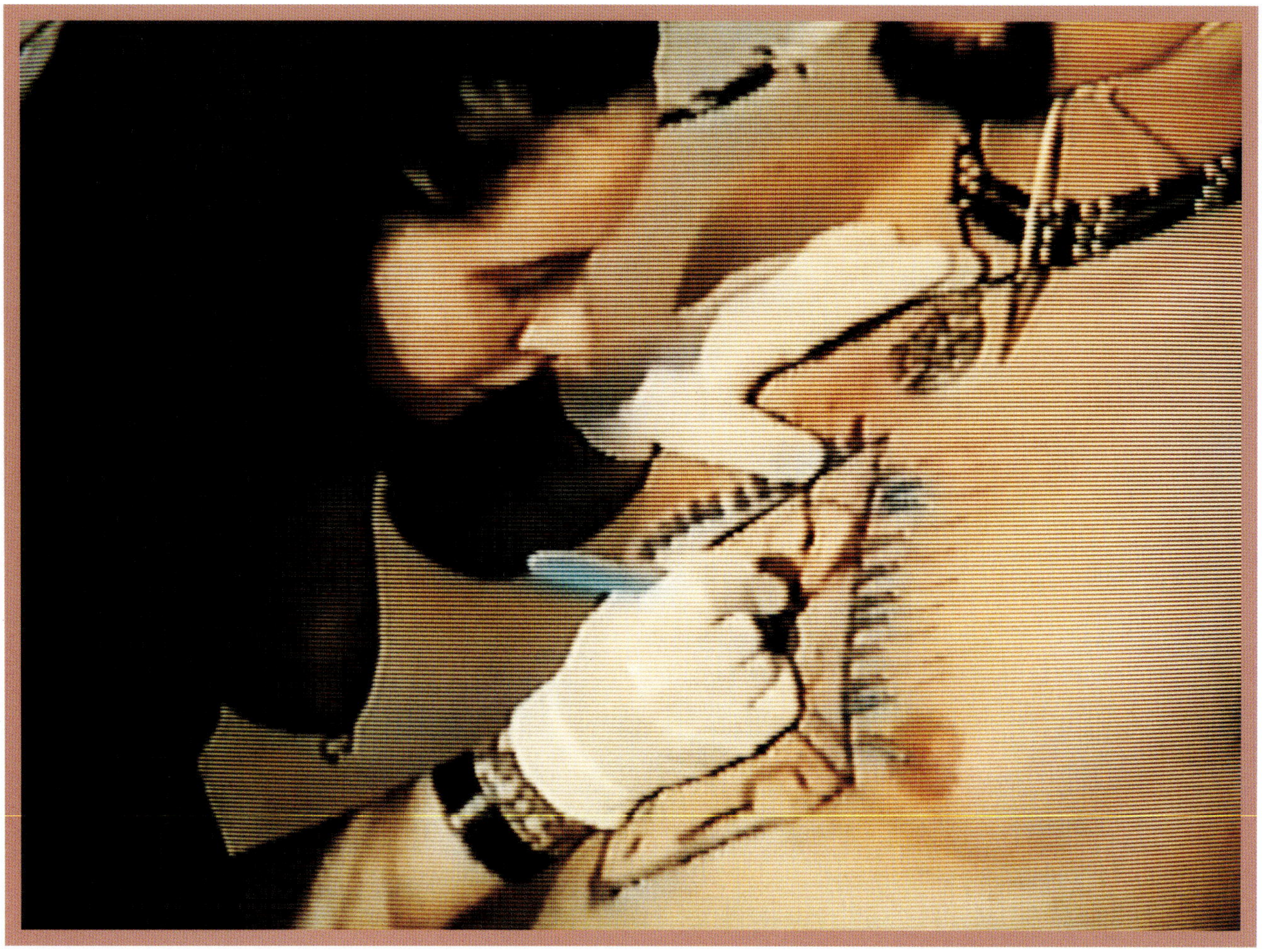

This is the squaw who initiates him; a visiting medicine woman. A witchy shaman. After years of progress, the screaming bat ground by biker tattoo artists into her strong back has become an angel in full flight—the only cost was her pain and humiliation.

She is the serene, softly-strong stitcher of invisibly wounded flesh. Opener of holes. Drainer of wounds. Prober of orifices. Whore of redemption. Queen mother of gutter madonnas. An elegant and fecund venus with amazon arms and praying mantis thighs.

She has smiled on many an Indian, seeking out the rare brave; offering the gift of her strength to the worthy. The selfish, imperfect worship they offer as reward cannot match the pleasant sight of their own blood dispersing in orderly waves.

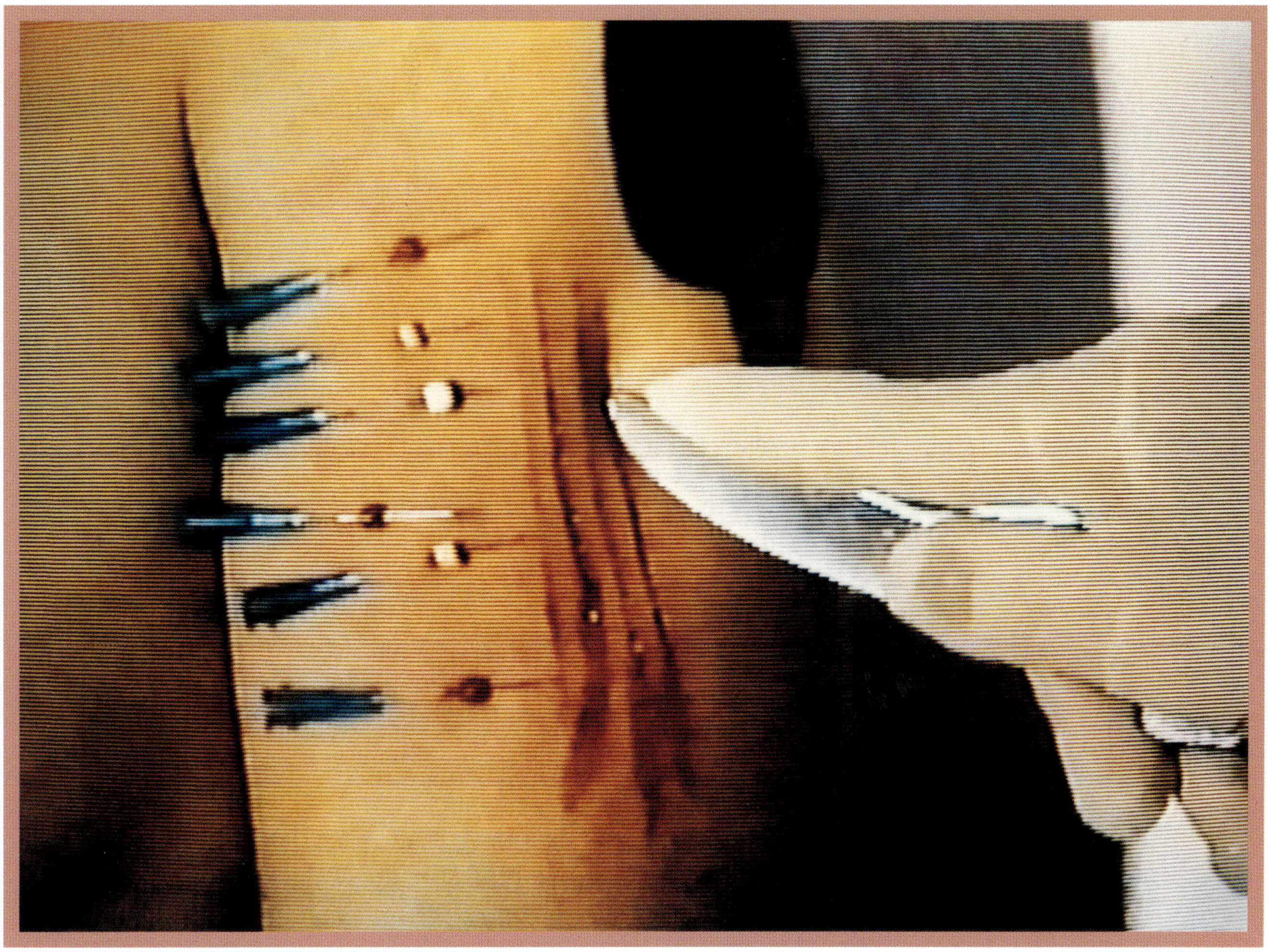

Now, that's Daddy's buck knife. And it hurts.

After the first taste of freedom every phantom wound begging to be born is finally rent and pouring gold-crimson from its tousled open maw, all infinity's treasures frolicking through the atmosphere, every thread now informed with the fire that must be shit out before any may rise through that loveless gate between us and pure static electricity.

This is our new testament, superceding all others:

Every time she forces open a door between the sticky pores of his flesh, his body shudders with the headlong thrust of his spirit trying to surf its way on the pounding blood waves of his heart, frantically seeking the limitless space outside reverberating with the one-second-off vibrations of an ethereal nether sphere where crueler angels wait, patient in their loving fury, instruments of infallible joy gleaming with sun-spot measure.

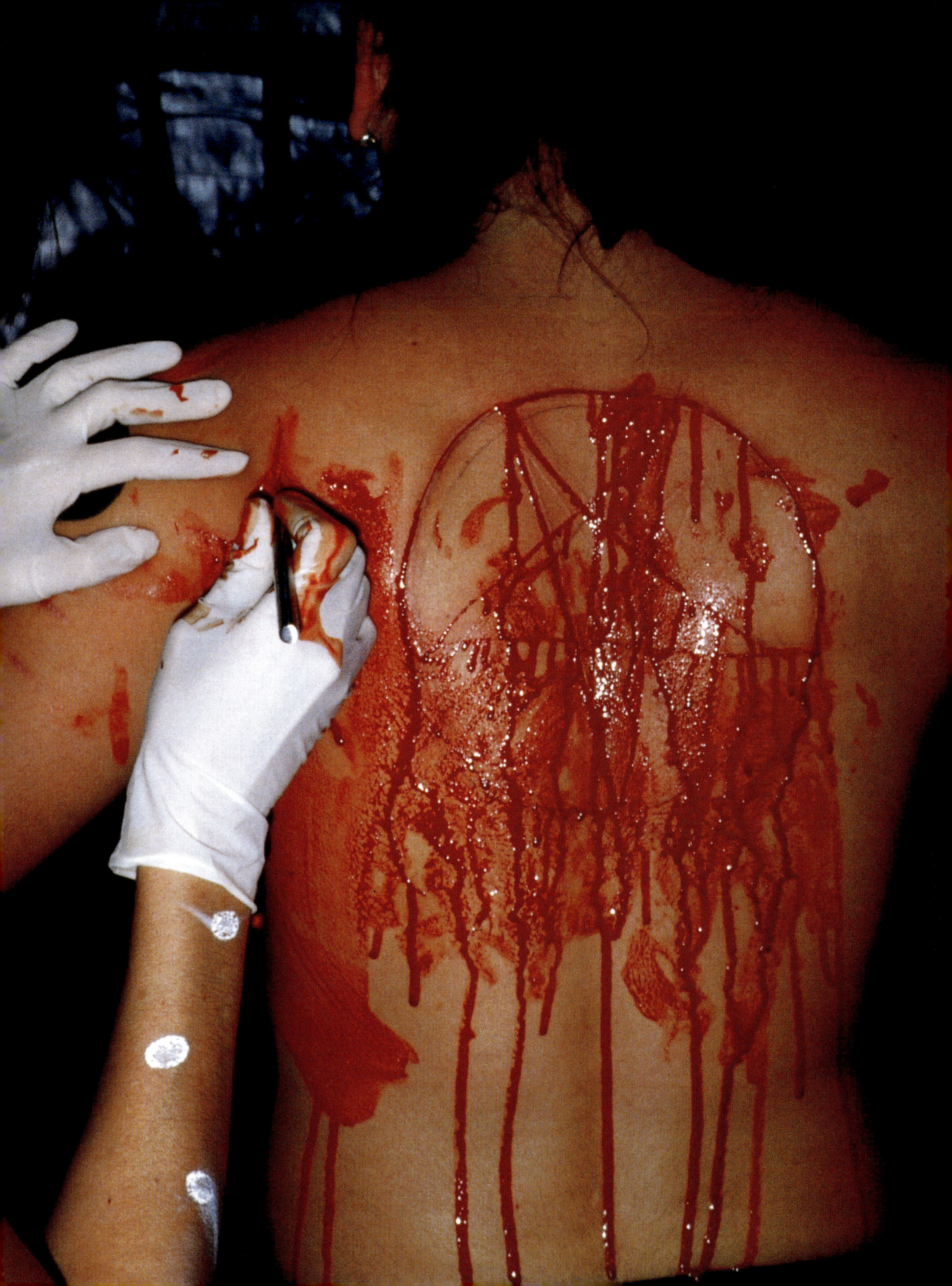

Meet Rebecca, Lilith, Eve, Lucifer's adopted daughters as well as mighty works of Jehovah. He drinks from their vials seven times and kisses their waists, hard with golden girdles. He cringes in the apex of their witchy circle as his air is sucked away, and on the altar they exercise power over the discreet orbits of certain atoms, white storm rising from the pit of endocrine plexus. Cold ladies of idle manipulation, are thee all Mystery, or her handmaidens only?

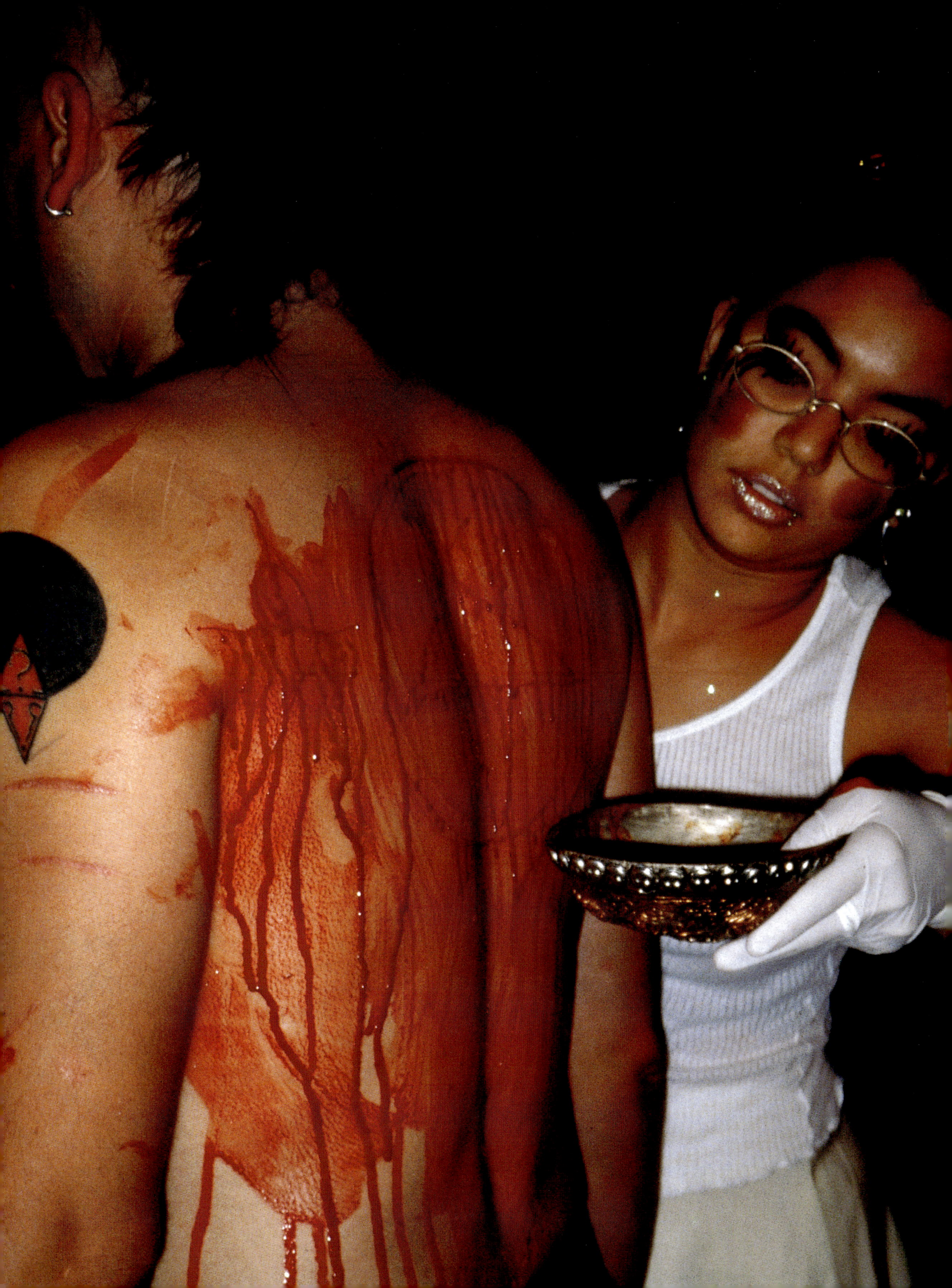

Our Lady Of The Perpetually Open Wound douses her narrow eyes with the red syrup that gathers between his legs. Our Lady Of The Virtual Thirst kisses the black scabs bridging the perforated skin, chewing them like beetles plucked from a savage veldt until they dissolve across her fat, provoked tongue. In an unregenerate vision no more profane than the slow crawl of time, a realm of a thousand crosses distinguishes itself from the static, each of them ready to embrace him with their pale, simple arms and potent, intimate conspiracy.

Taught to sin by fallen and compassionate angels, he has rode the arc's razor into the bowels of the lamb, and fears not the looming spool of the fourth seal, its brute ornate glamour precise and inviting. His tutors are a barbaric host, an army of soft limbs and voices that palliate their infernal serenity with sentimental ardor.

None of you can kiss me as sweetly as this splintered wood, just hand me over in your studied elegance and pour me the vinegar that is the fierceness of your wrath, conduct me with blood and love into a clear state of perdition.

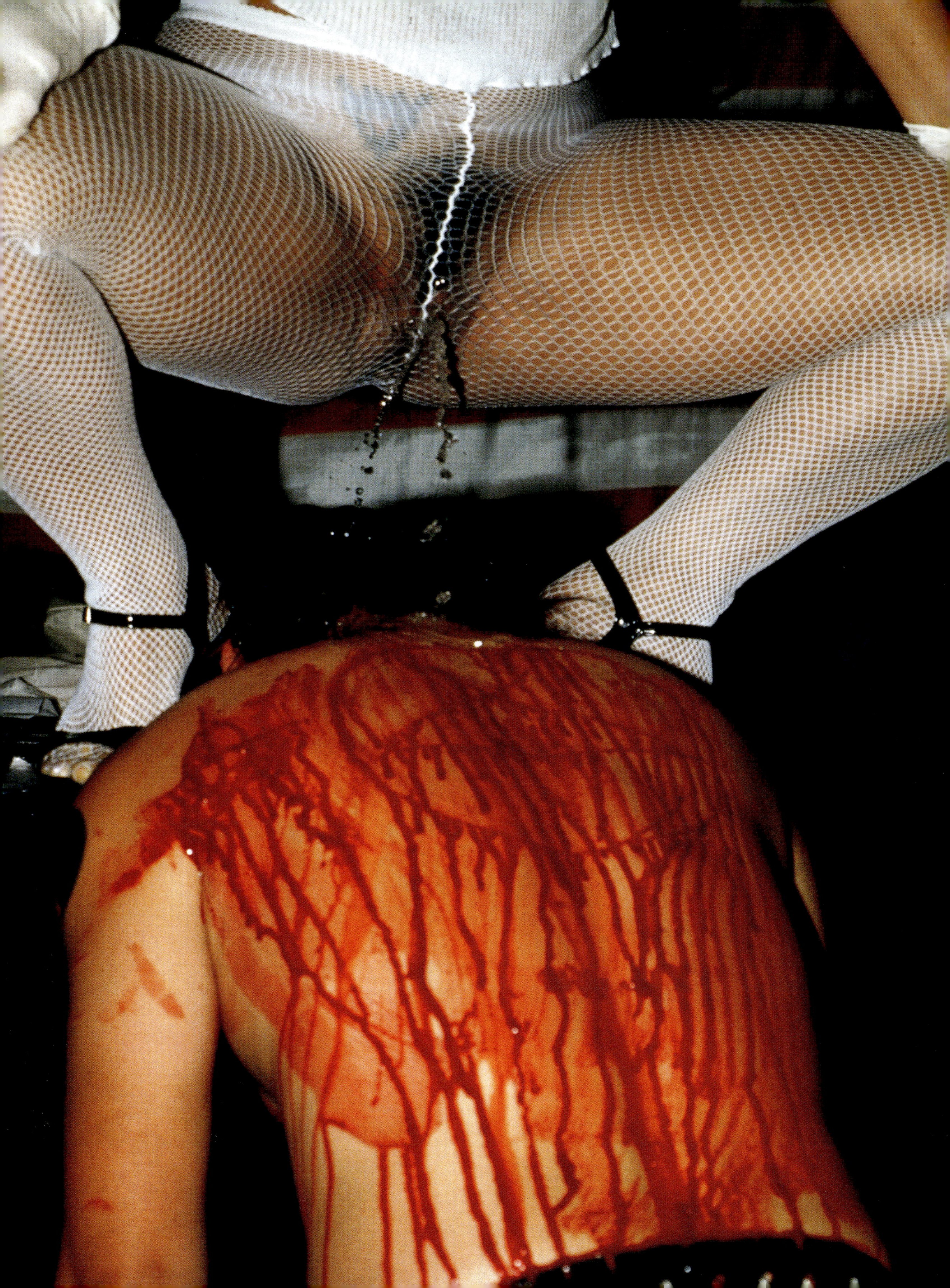

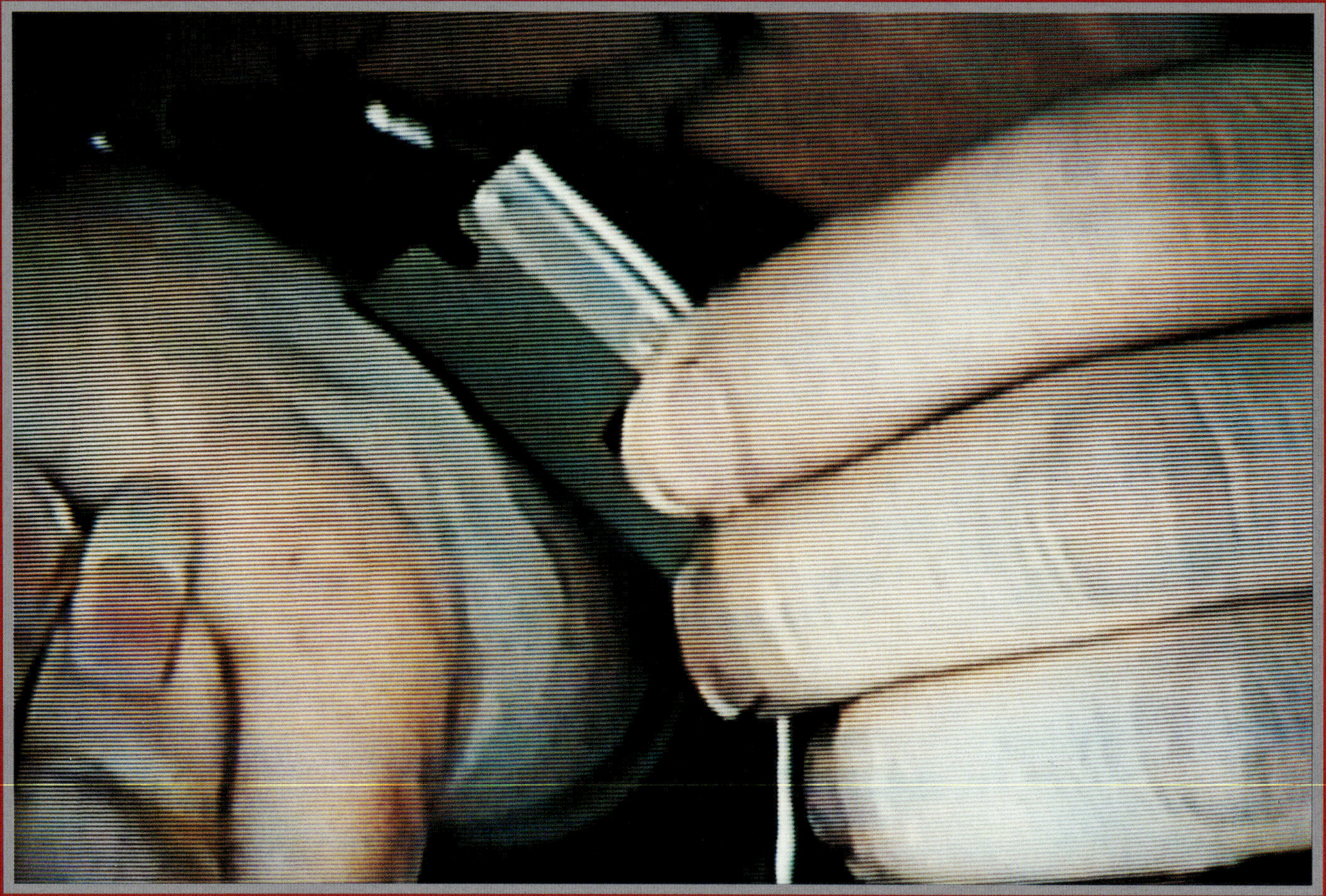

Our breed
does not breed
our breed

bitch's blood
loser's blood
madwoman's blood
thief's blood
faggot's blood
fool's blood
outcast's blood
victim's blood

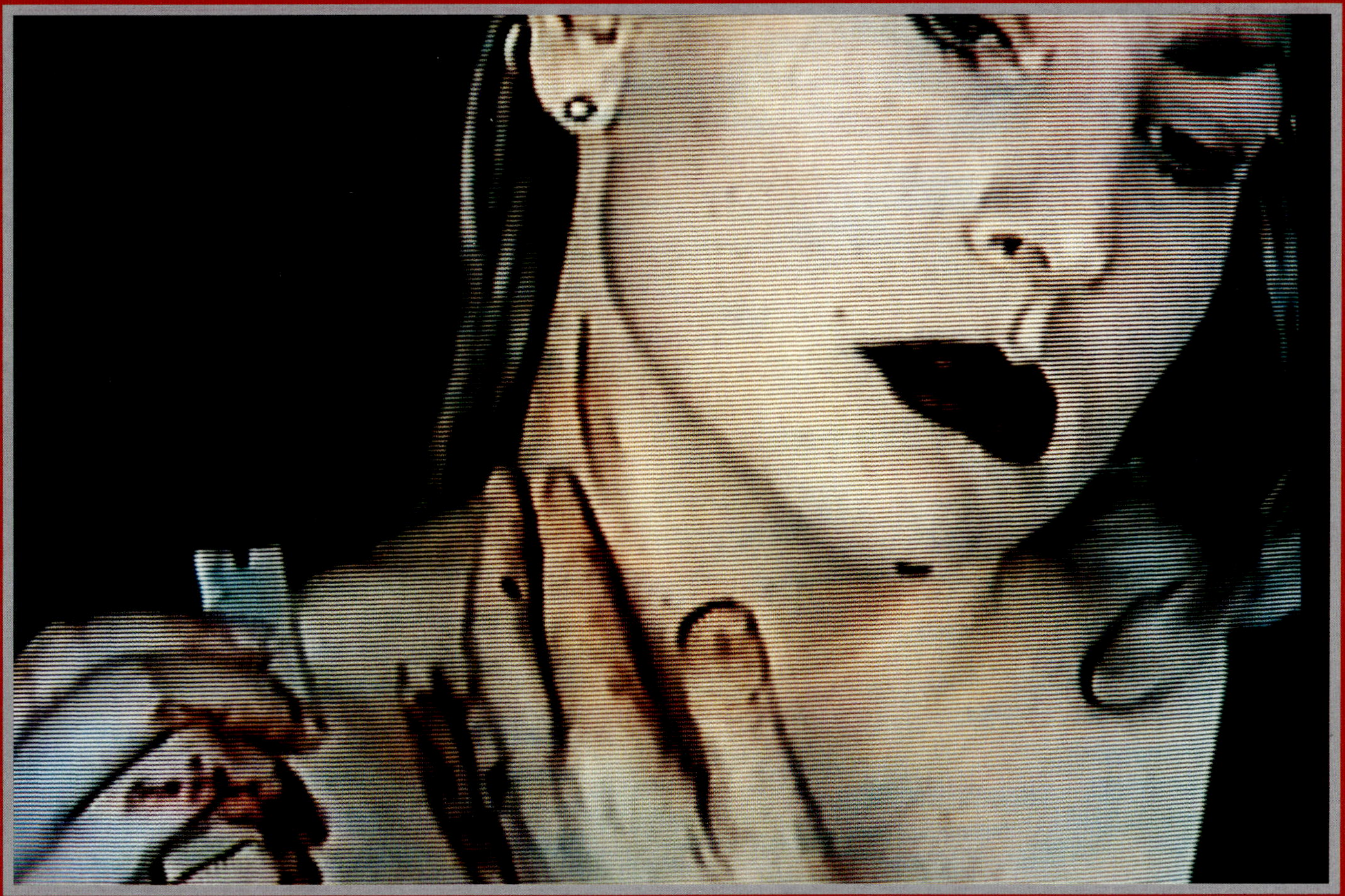

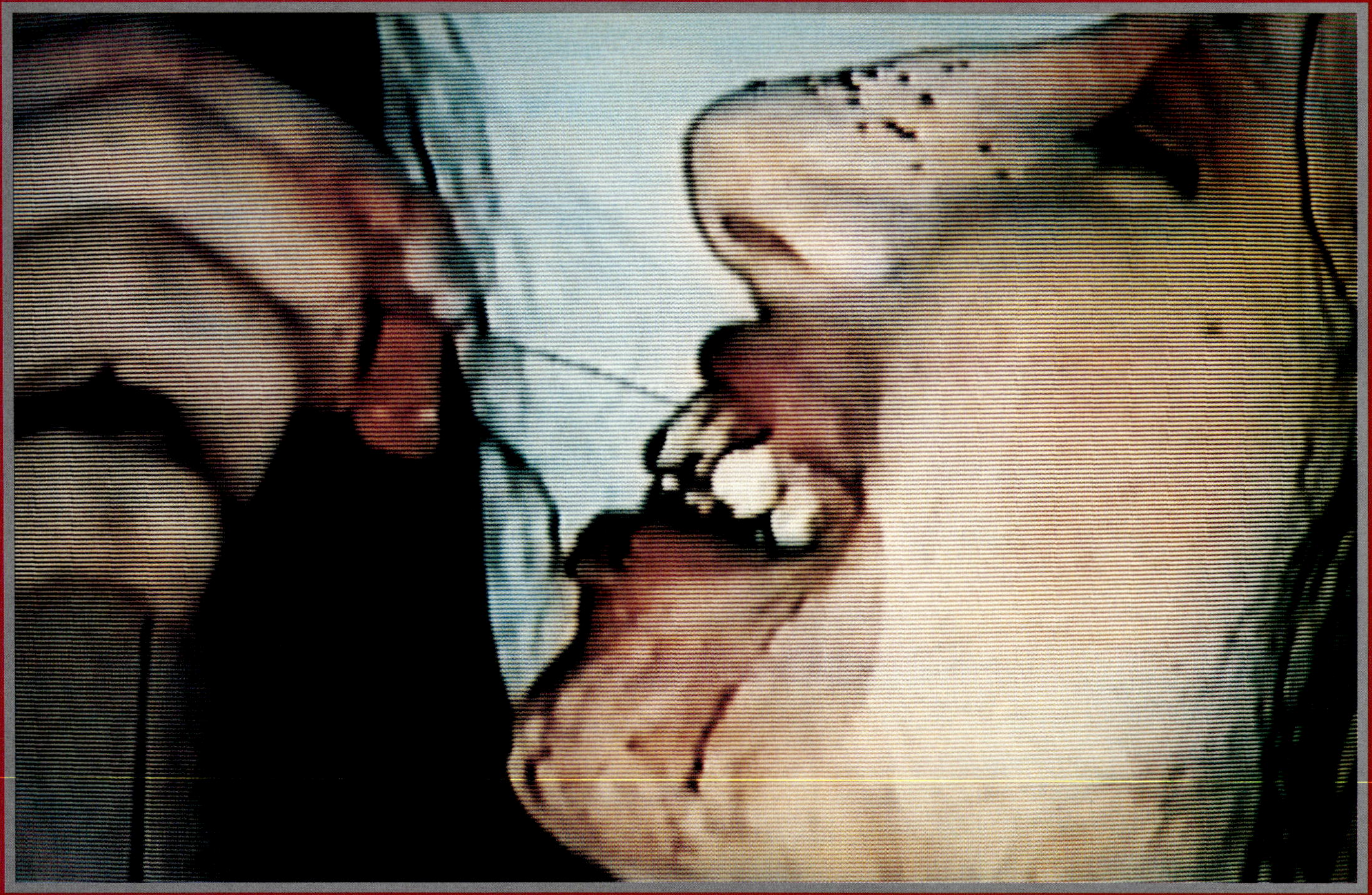

It's all sacred. Even if so cold mere moments out of the vein.

Though some prefer it that way. Imagining it safer, that germs die quickly in the open air. Or for the ironic distance that precludes the terror of unrehearsed intimacy; a retreat into crypto-medical fetishism. Place settings for a well-mannered mayhem.

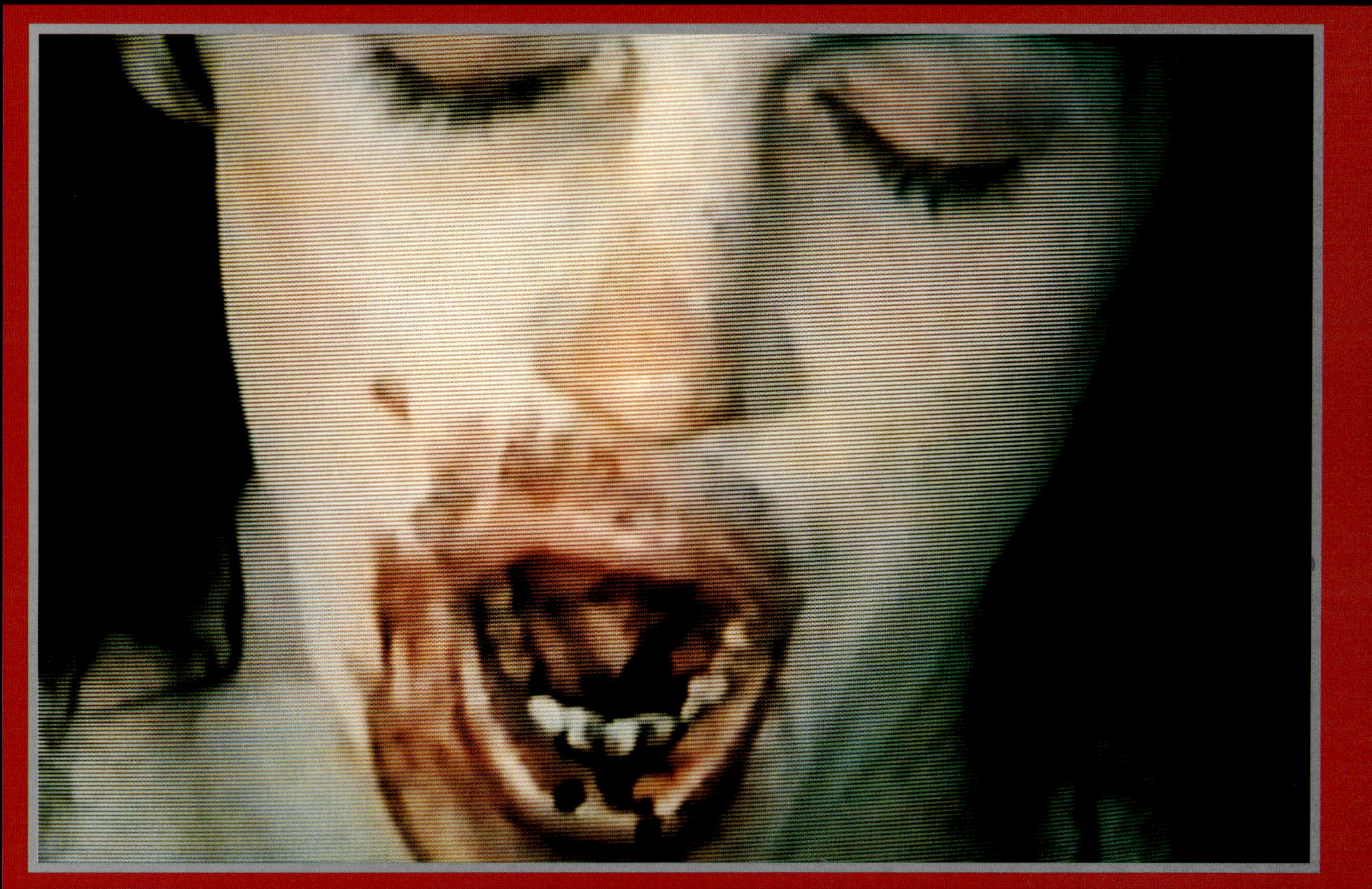

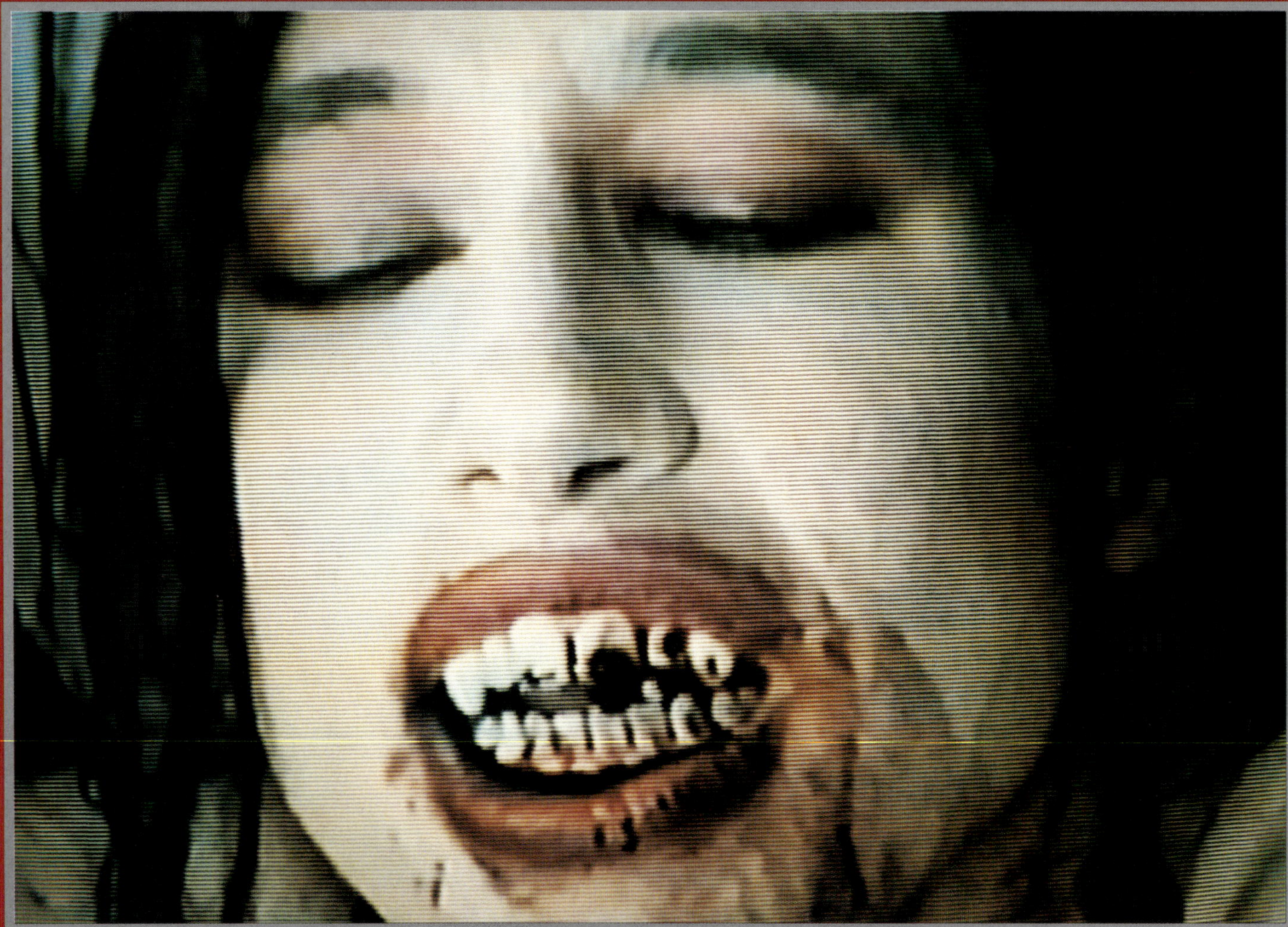

But I don't care.

Punch a door into my throat. Make it mean something.

And then tell me some bed-time stories:

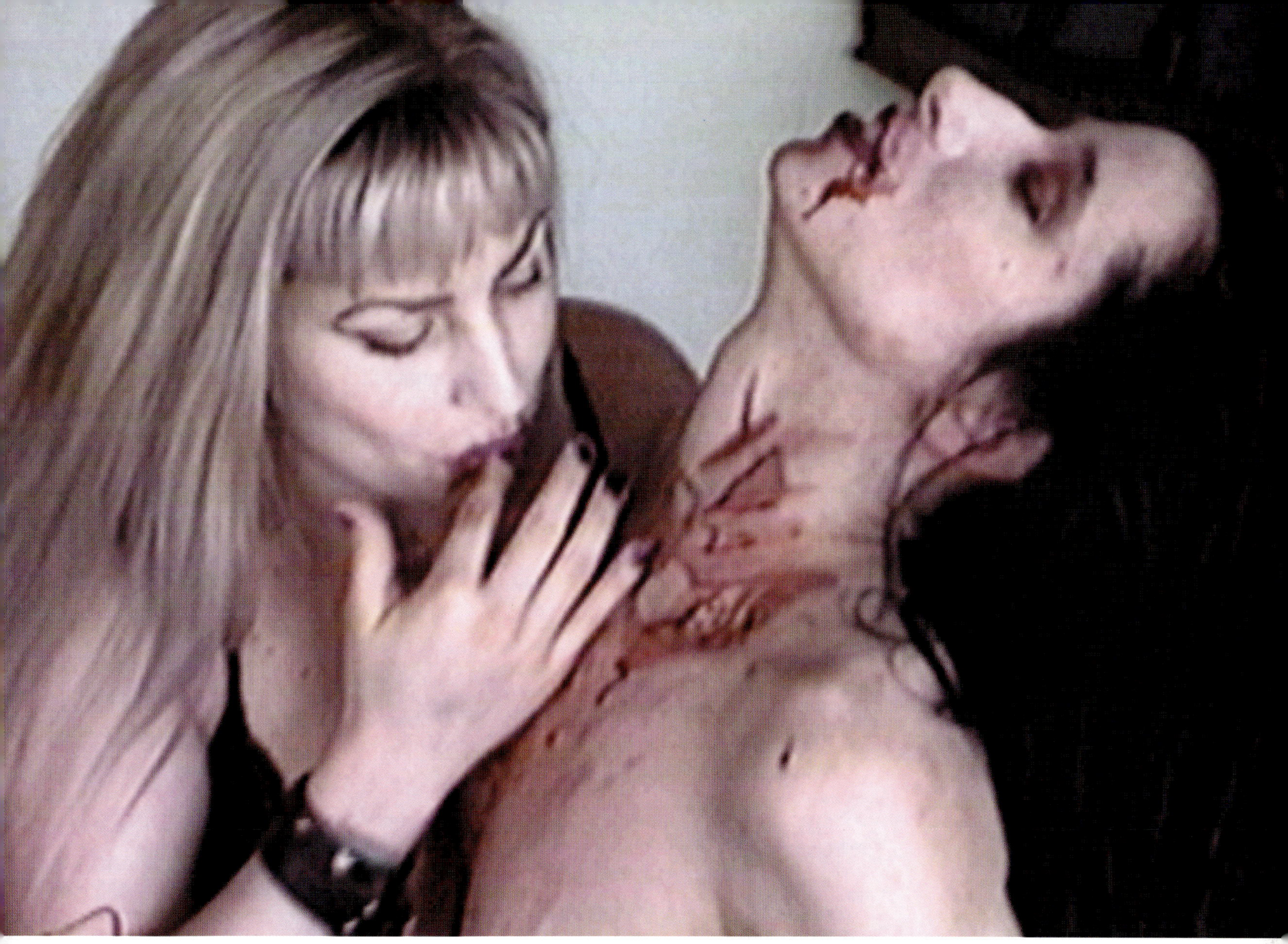

Carmilla comes to visit us on the thirteenth day of my twenty-first year. Of obscure and noble lineage, she immediately impresses my father with her impeccable manners, and is invited to be our house guest until her uncle returns from an extended business trip.

"She first makes love to me on the cellar's dirt floor, cutting both my wrists then clamping them together with the sticky paste of their blood and her saliva now turning to cement hardening to shackles that she draws above my head so my naked chest, the leather and bone coffin jailing my heart might be bitten open. As my pulse slows she convulses and comes, a wolf with a weeping cunt. It will be the most simple of our games.

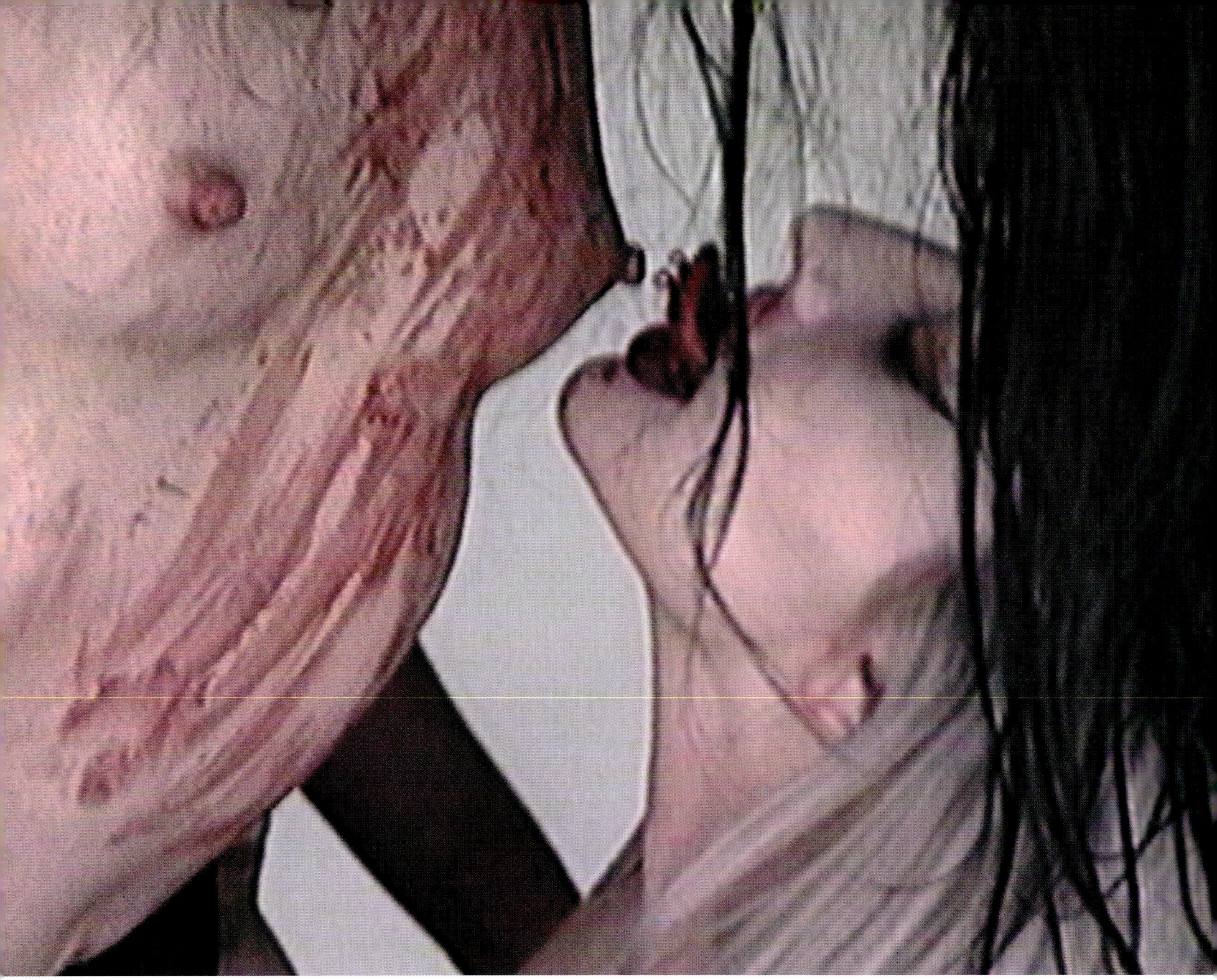

Now I become langorous and weak; I despise the daylight, which knows no compromise or ambiguity. My appetite has undergone a wrenching transformation, and there is no wine that does not taste puerile, no meat fresh enough to envigor my veins. I fall into spells during the late afternoon, watching as the walls of my bed chamber, which I am loathe to leave, run red with blood. I tremble to orgasm during these faints, waking wracked with sobs and rolling my eyes.

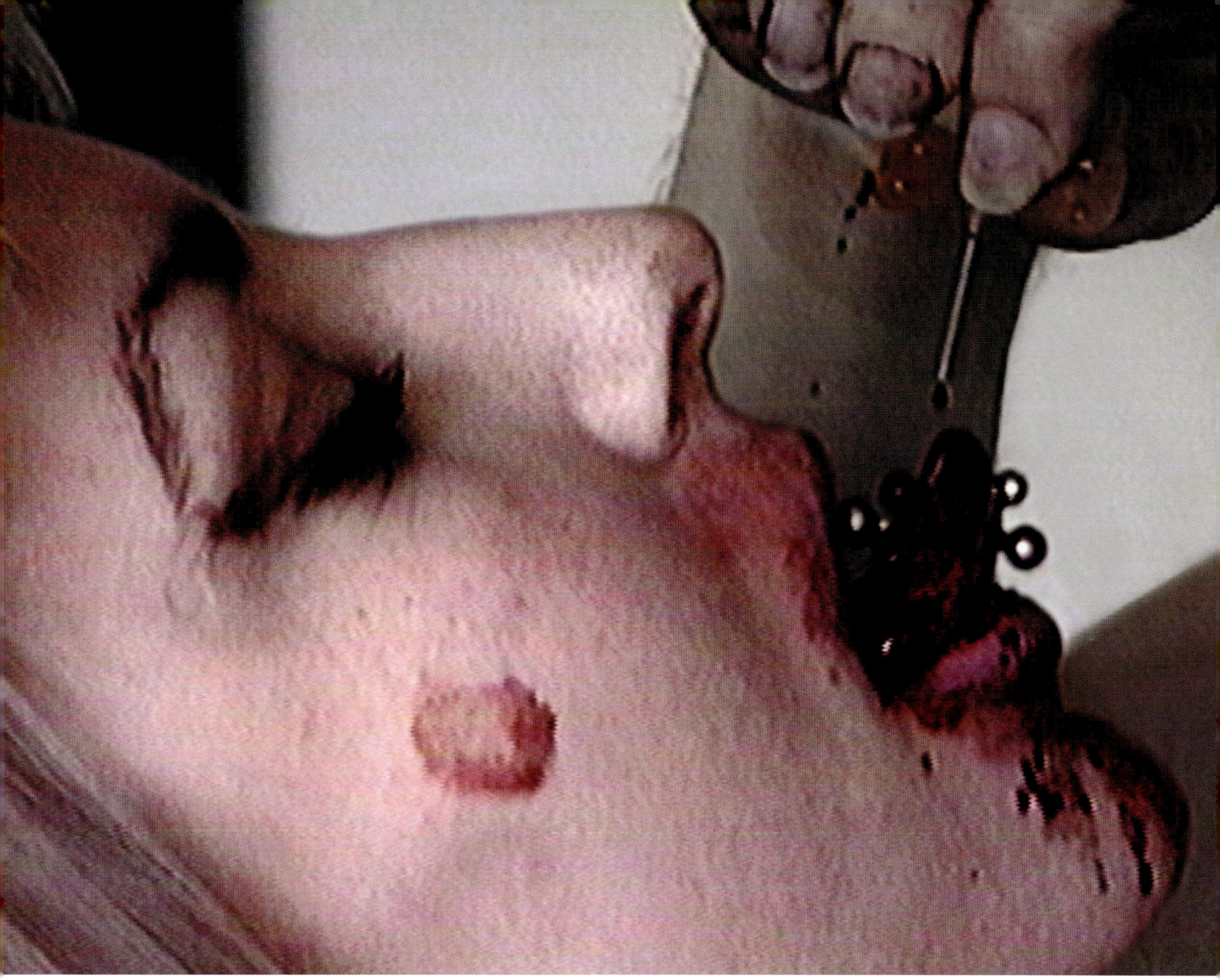

Carmilla says she is my sister but I know she is my shadow, a casual demon distracted by the diluted gleam of her own reflection. I am her drug. she is my Pandemonium. Our death will be lucid and plain. Father could never understand. He will have to be seen to, so our plan is not thwarted."

In her favorite masturbation fantasy, she is Elizabeth Bathory's first victim, Countess and whore tenderly exchanging blood virginities, the sacrifice of giving up her life made up for by the knowledge in those last conscious seconds that a madwoman and serial killer will idolize her forever as First, as with tender speculation and wide eyes the Countess oversees that the mean twice-sold flesh is hung and drained until marbled like the finest meat, even as her expression of sad orgasm at the moment of death sinks forever deeply into a hungry black heart chosen to power a macabre reign that will inspire myth and history. Much of history is determined by whores, she always thinks as she comes.

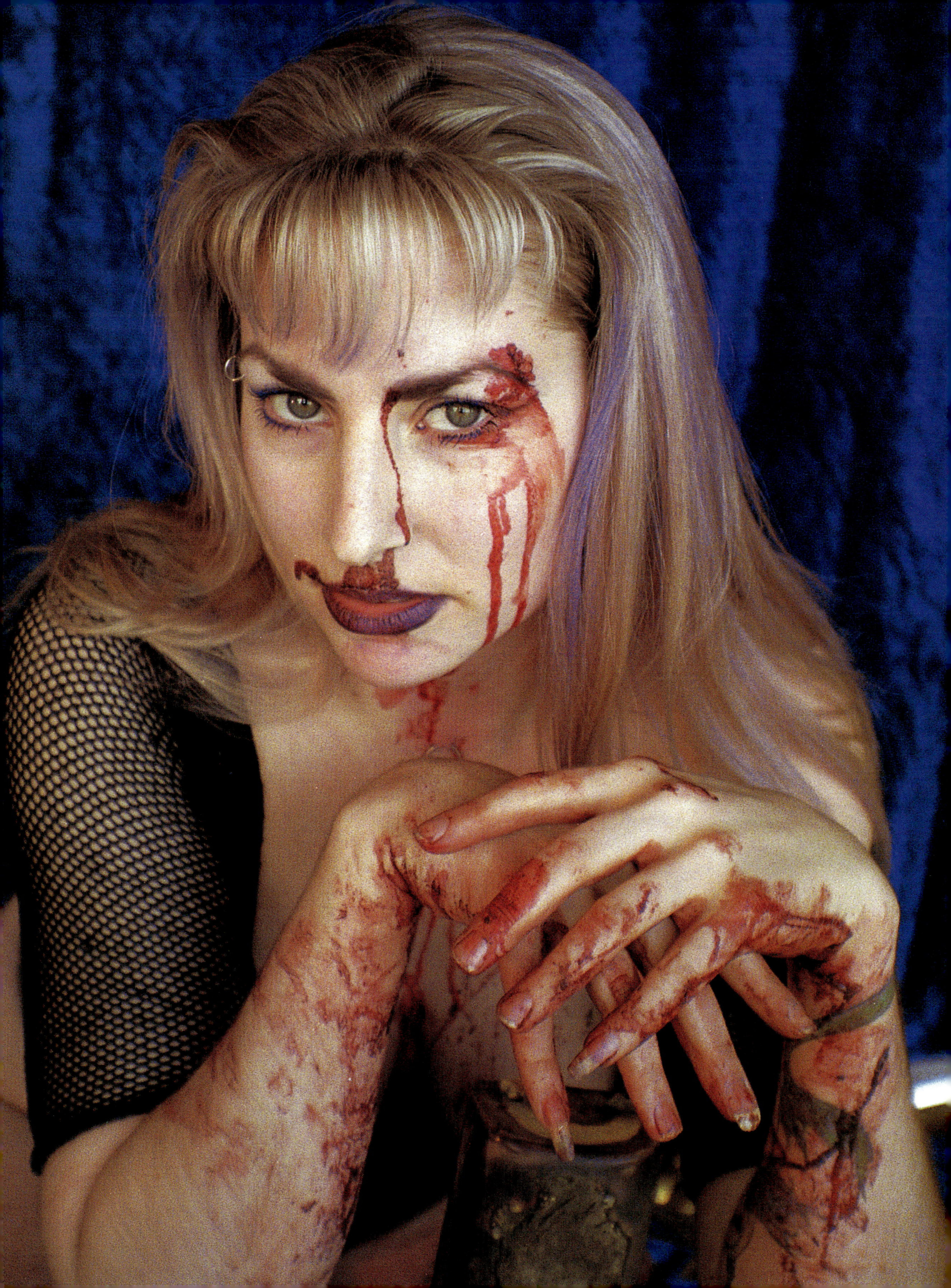

Today's Sermon: Is Hunger Innocent?

So hang the mismatched black letters in their Venetian tracks, nestled to the side of the treacherously rough-hewn stone staircase that leads to: still, tepid water in cold marble troughs **that** leads to: knee against wood **that** leads to: a eunuch's judgement—

This is what a bad girl you are.

Fuck all sermons.

Desecrate all uniforms. I will stain them with my want, your lust, fate's ejaculation. I am a creature born of my hungers, and I fuck as I feed. I pass all poisons in the créme of my excitement.

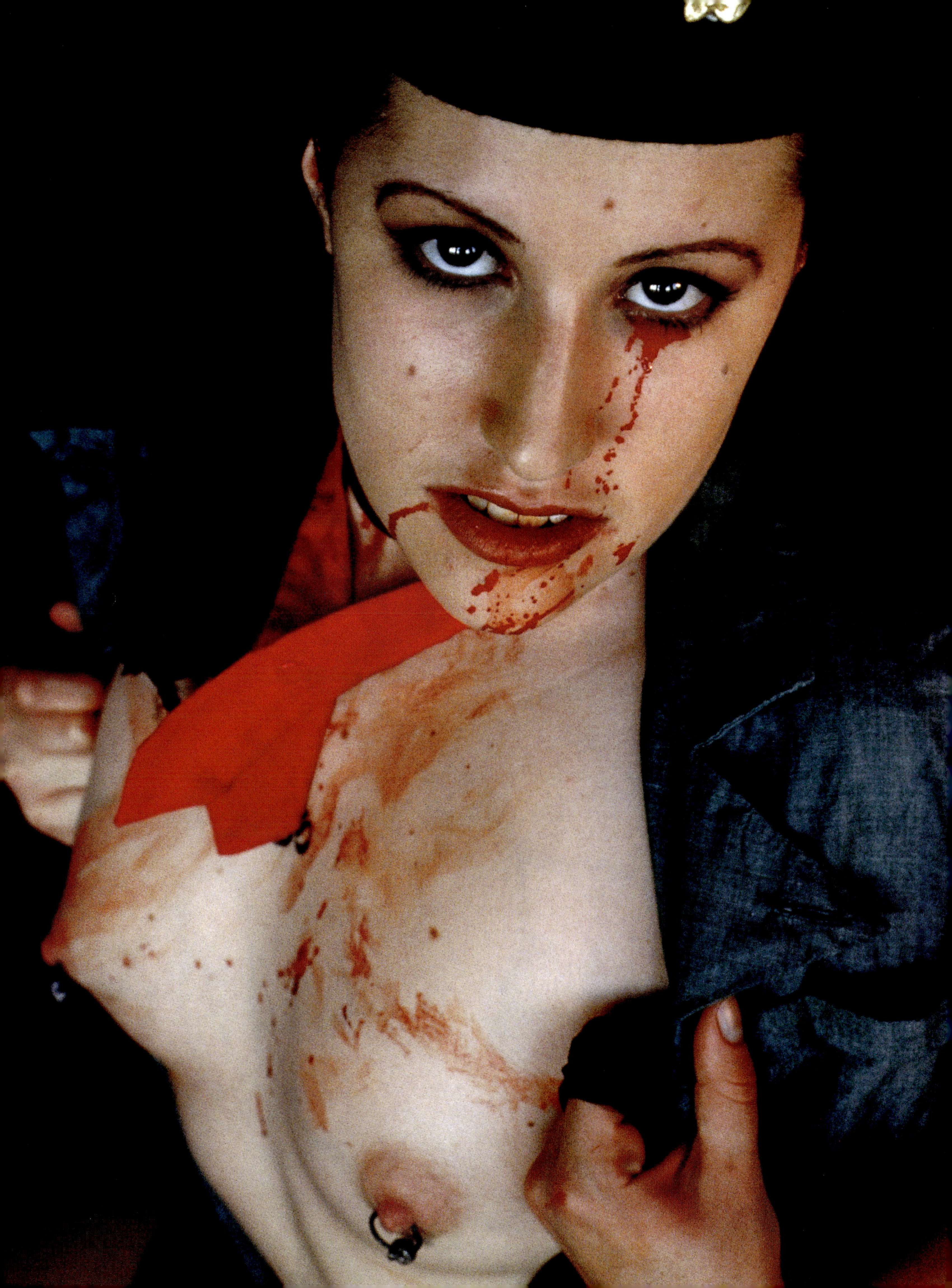

Turn the mirrors against the wall
and give me your skin
I swear you won't even feel it open
jack off for me now jack off
forever
Or at least until your nerves stop sparkling
and your cock is soft and raw
I hate those people on the street
I hate exposing these tender wounds to the open air
Risking the infection of the mundane
I'd rather stay in here and play with you.

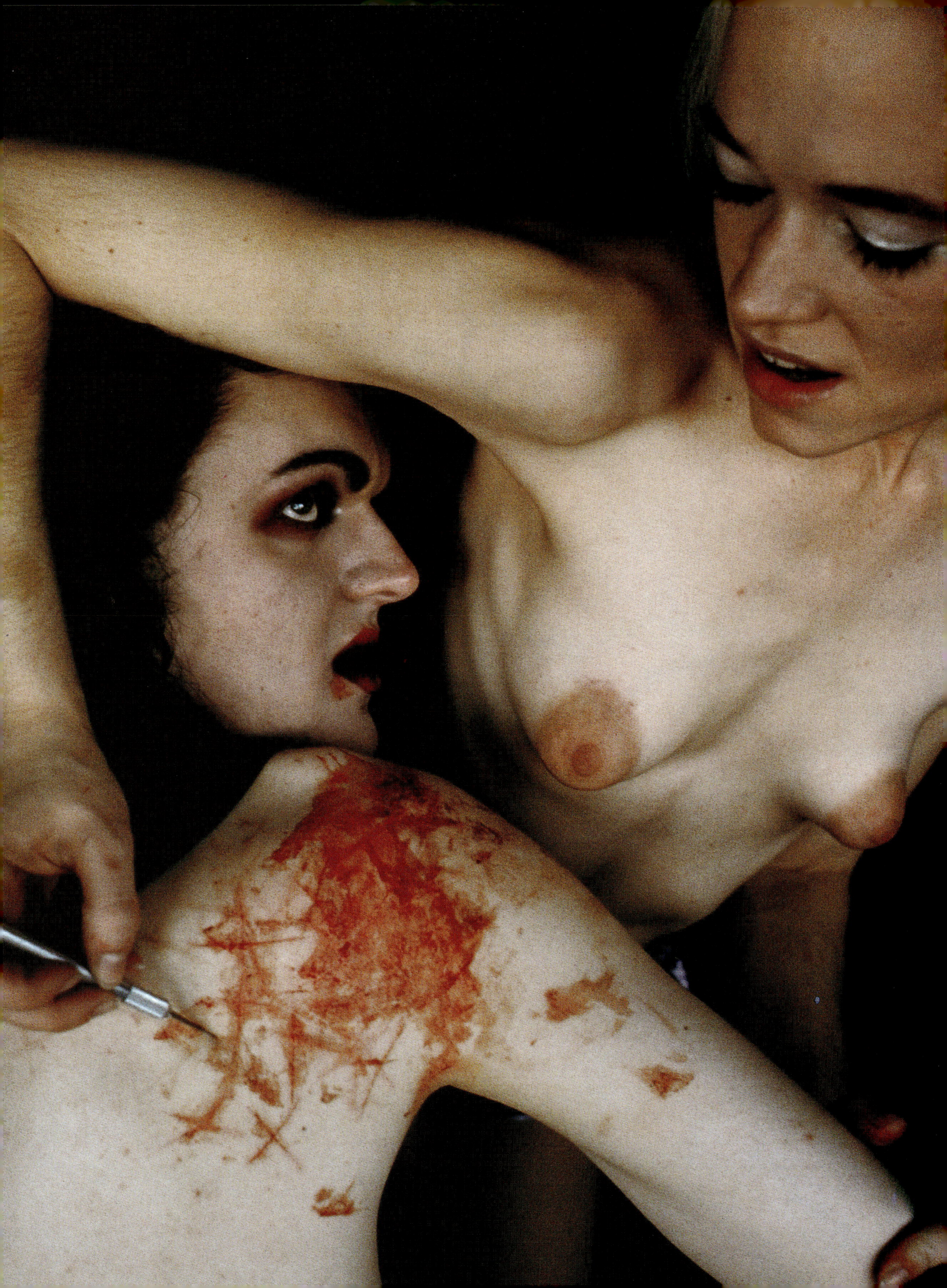

Isn't this quite a large needle?
Aren't these razors particularly shiny?
Isn't this better than watching TV?
At least for a little while...
Tell me when you can't
Feel it anymore
So we can start
Really having fun.

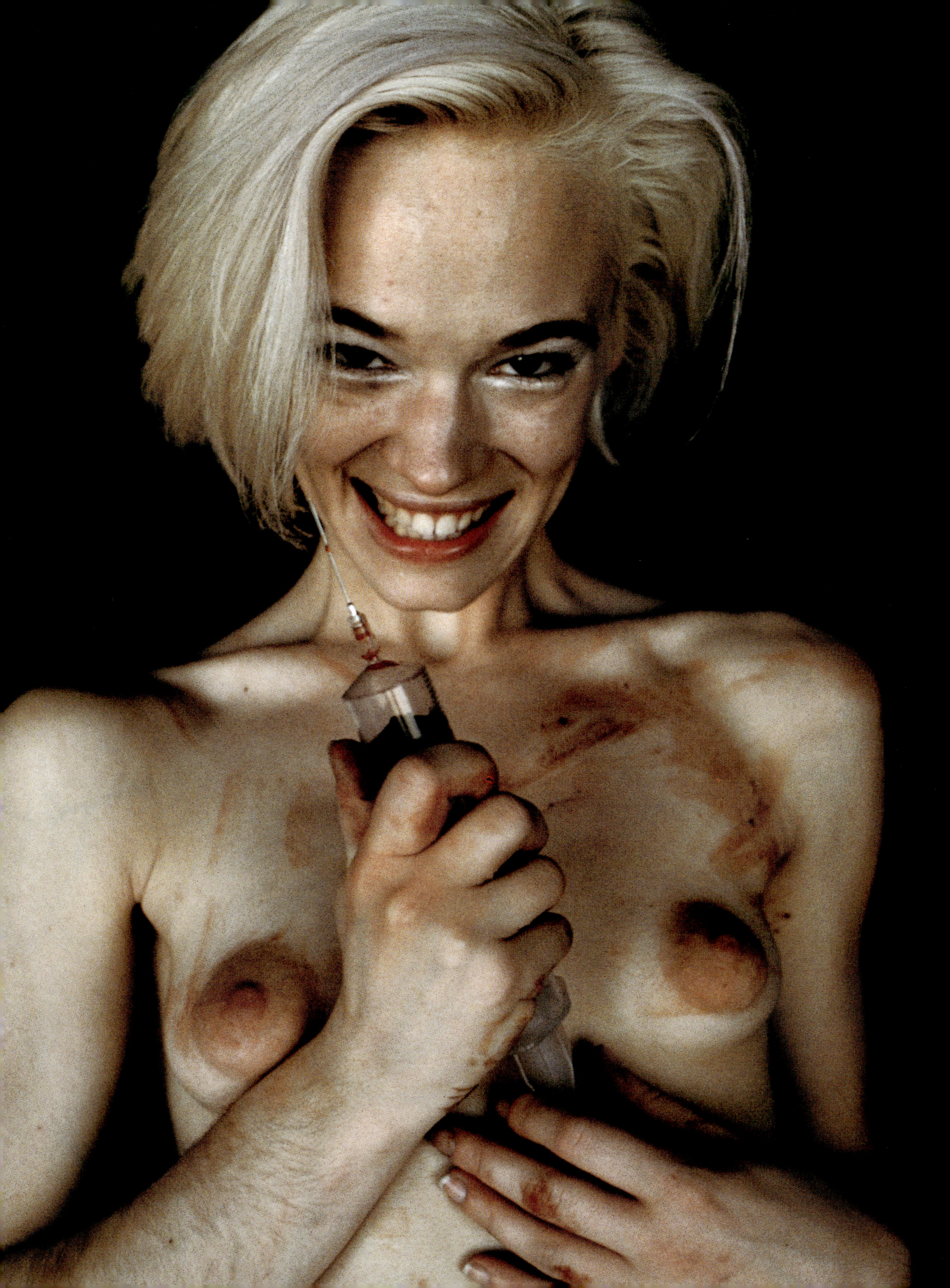

We are wed sometime past midnight on the blasted playa; the only other life out here is microscopic.

We are wed in the flat shadows of hastily strung arc lights that stain skin blue with their glare. Drugged eyes burn white from the restless crowd of sybarites that mills beyond the safety rope, self-possessed hipsters who have wandered out to the Nevada desert on this Labor Day weekend hoping to embrace some bizarre spectacle so they might return to their coffeehouses and crashpads wiser, more informed. More *cool.* Full of anecdotes.

They don't understand that the blood is about to come. We savor their innocence, making a last toast of it before taking up the marital cup. The spirits of slaughtered animals sing the bridal march at an aetheric frequency too sharp for human ears.

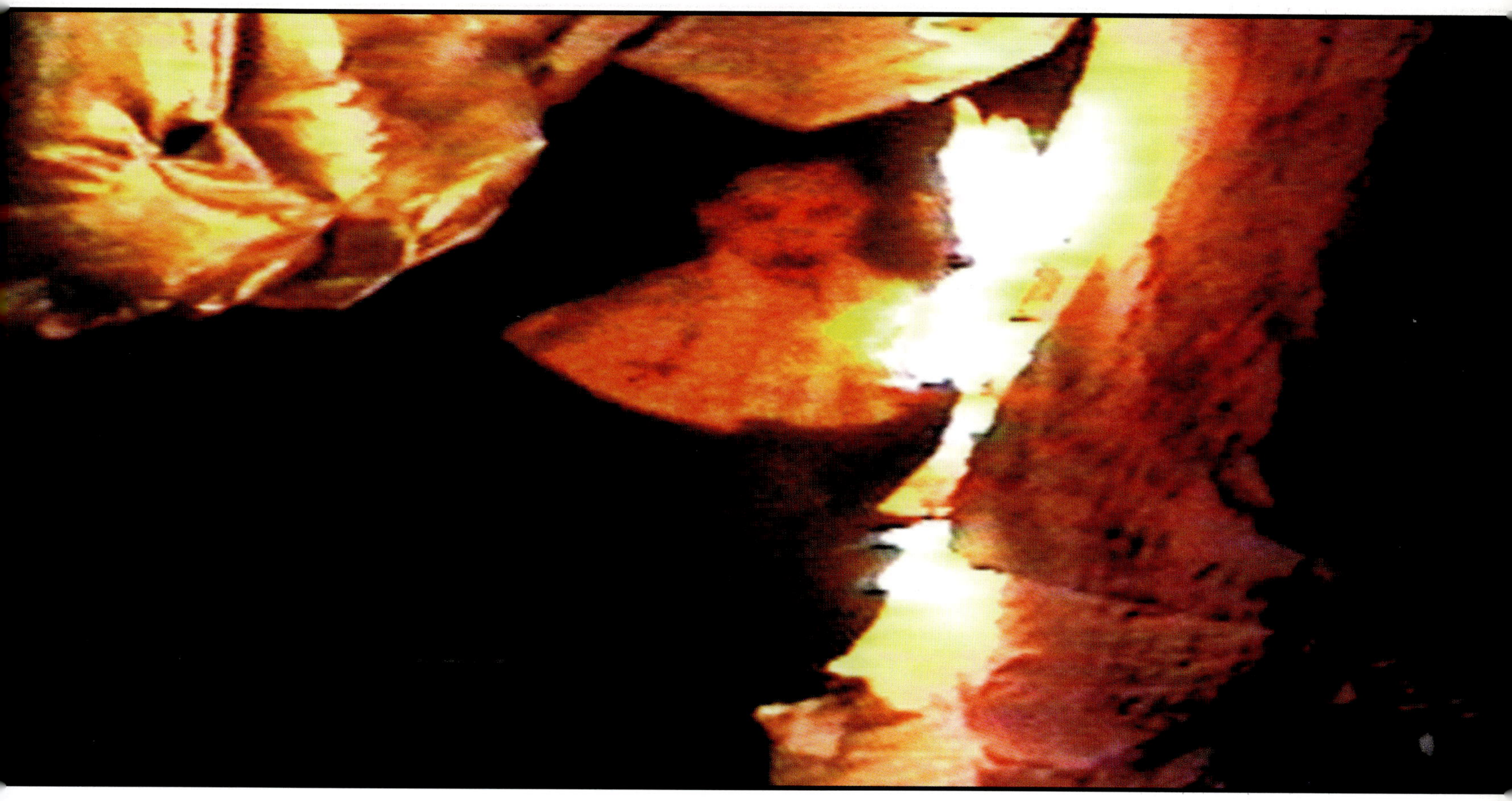

We are wed by a somnambulent cleric thin and pallorous, precise in his benediction, who wears arm-length black rubber gloves.

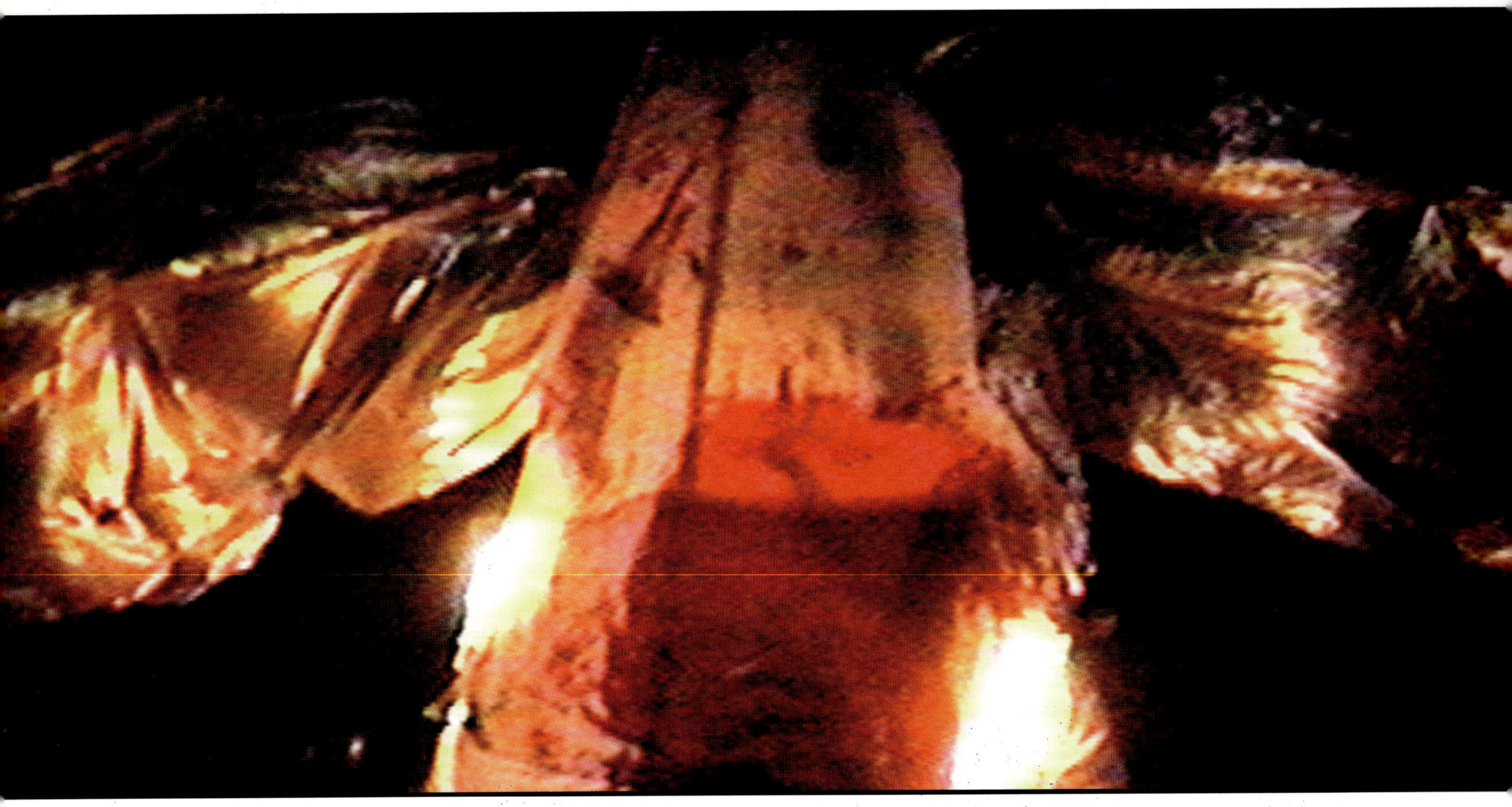

We are wed before a chickenwire angel stuffed with viscera, topped with the rotting fresh skull of a slaughtered steer, an admirable vessel beseeching possession by the restlessly whispering djinns that have slunk through the swirling lanes of desolate midnight breezes to offer their wedding gifts:

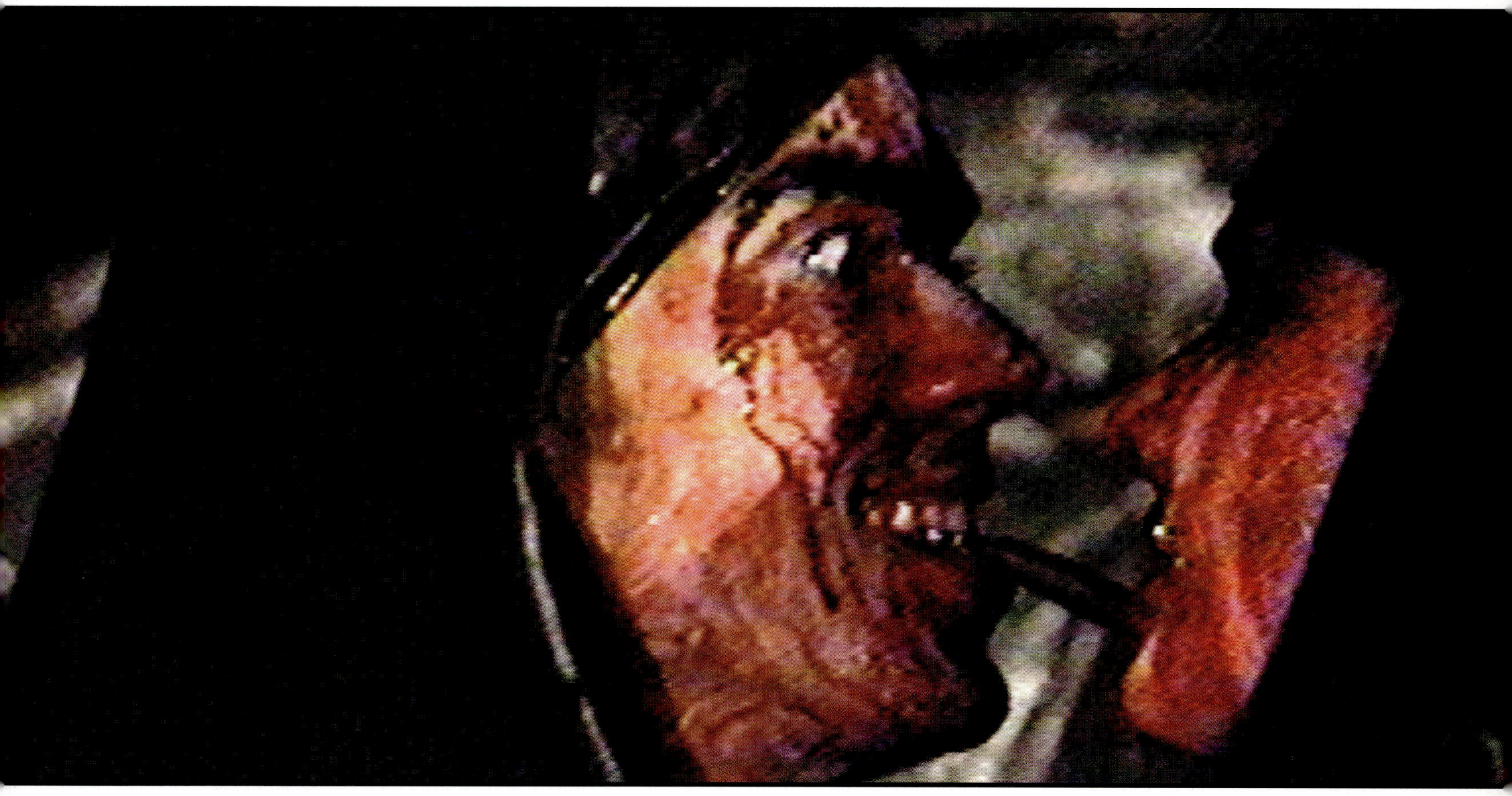

Carnivorism

(transmogrification of life into waste into life: the only true immortality)

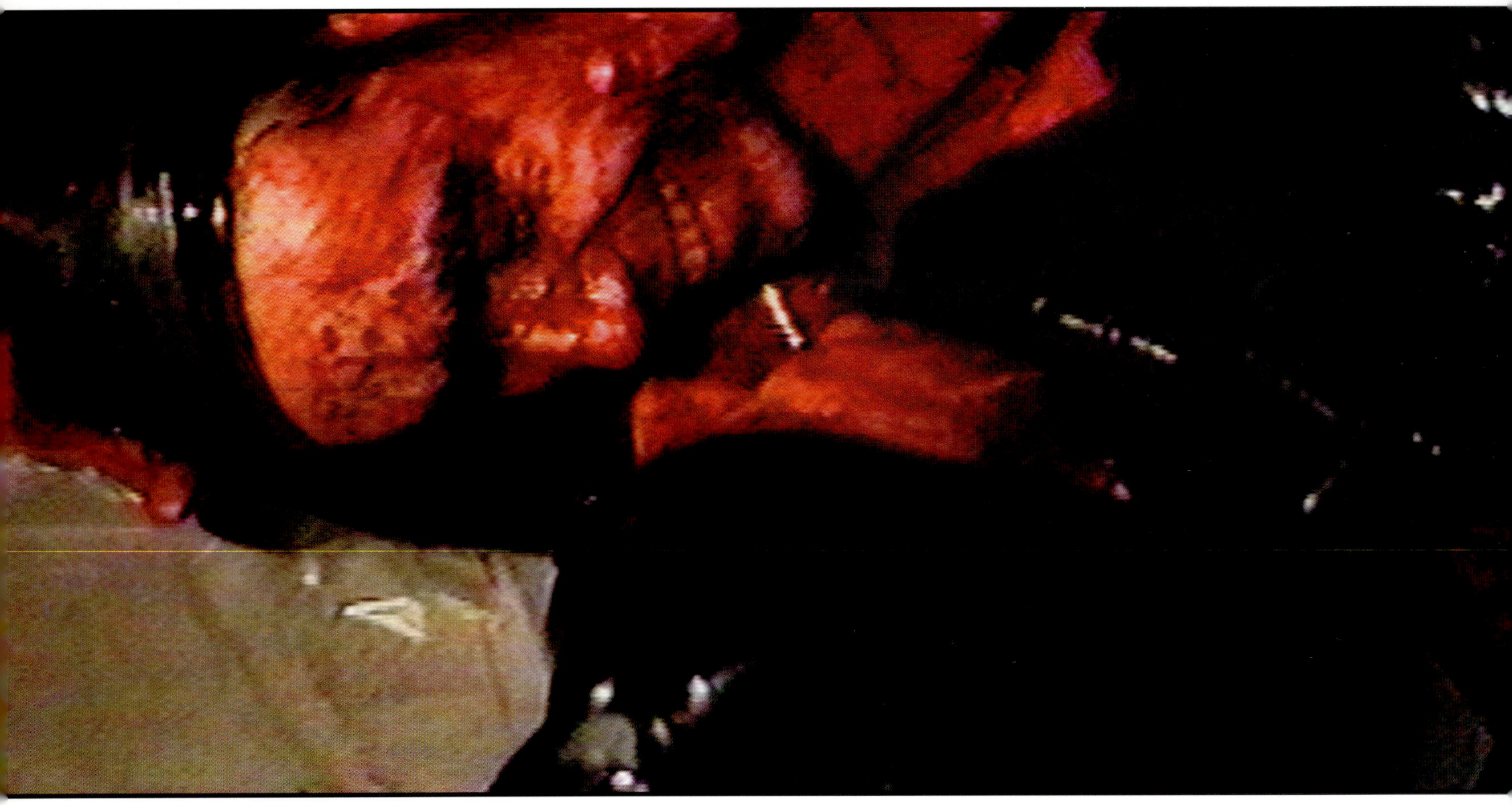

Mesmerism

(the power in your/my eyes)

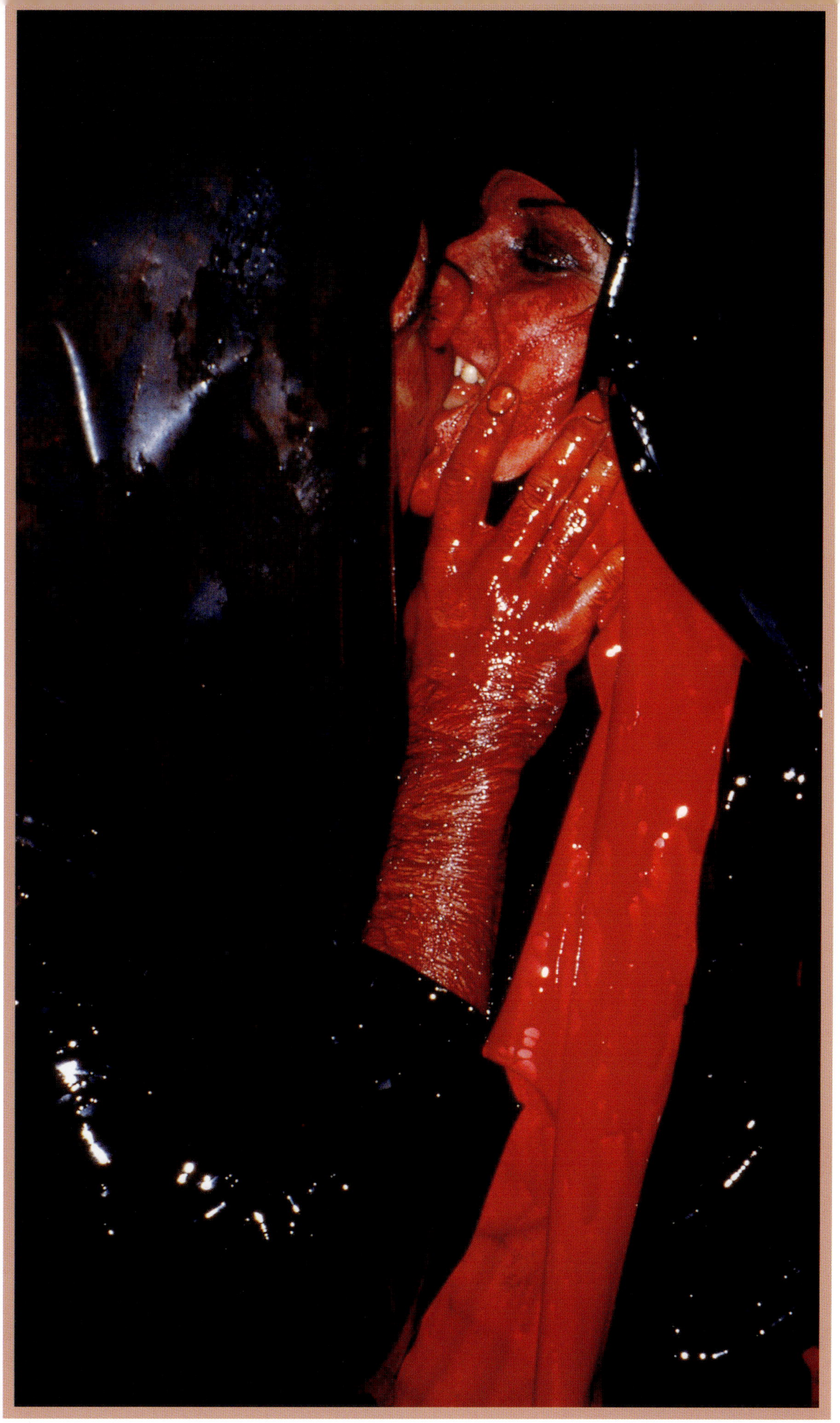

Omniscience

(hidden in the subtle celestial weaves suddenly standing out in relief against the clear and endless desert night)

The cleric sets the oil drums crammed with meat aflame; his blazing hand declares us one; the angel vomits its red approval on our heads, and we bathe in the putrifying waters of anonymously ended lives, souls destined for our dining board. Transported frozen in milk cartons out to the desert, and left to slowly melt until this moment. A shower for the Blood-Spattered Bride and her adoring mate.

As we embrace the cleric binds us together with a clear, strong hose, through which presently runs more blood, endless blood, as if from God's mighty heart itself. Eager to consummate but trapped in our elaborate gowns, we tumble down into the muddy red pool at our feet, sliding and rubbing and biting each other's lips.

The stink is phenomenal. Our lives are one.

Drugged and sleepless, the gathering of witnesses howls, as an insane muscian rends electrified piano wire with his teeth. A riderless motorcycle buzzes through our circle of white vapor and disappears again into the infinite distance of night.

The blood has become our second skin. It is draining into our pores: Spirits of slaughtered beasts forever trapped. Driving our hearts.

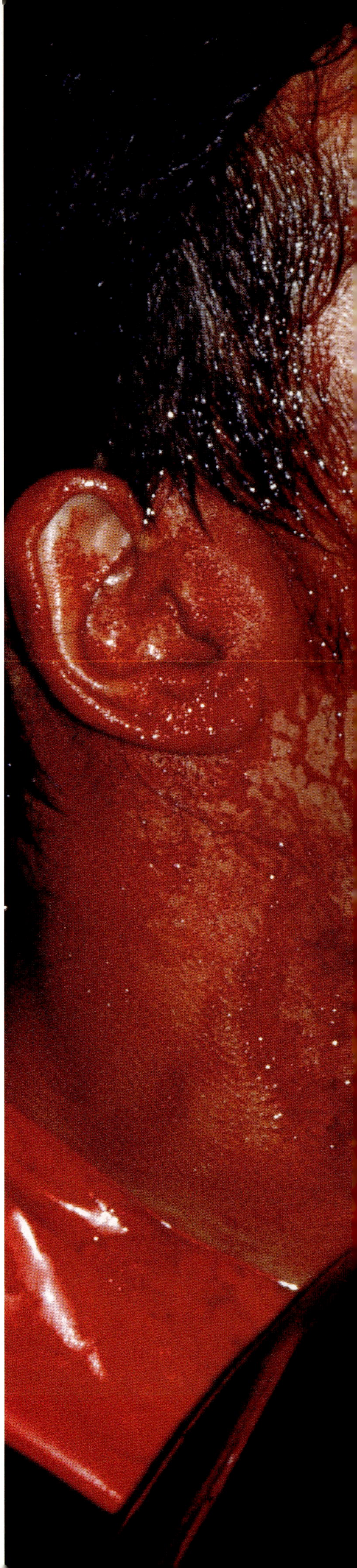

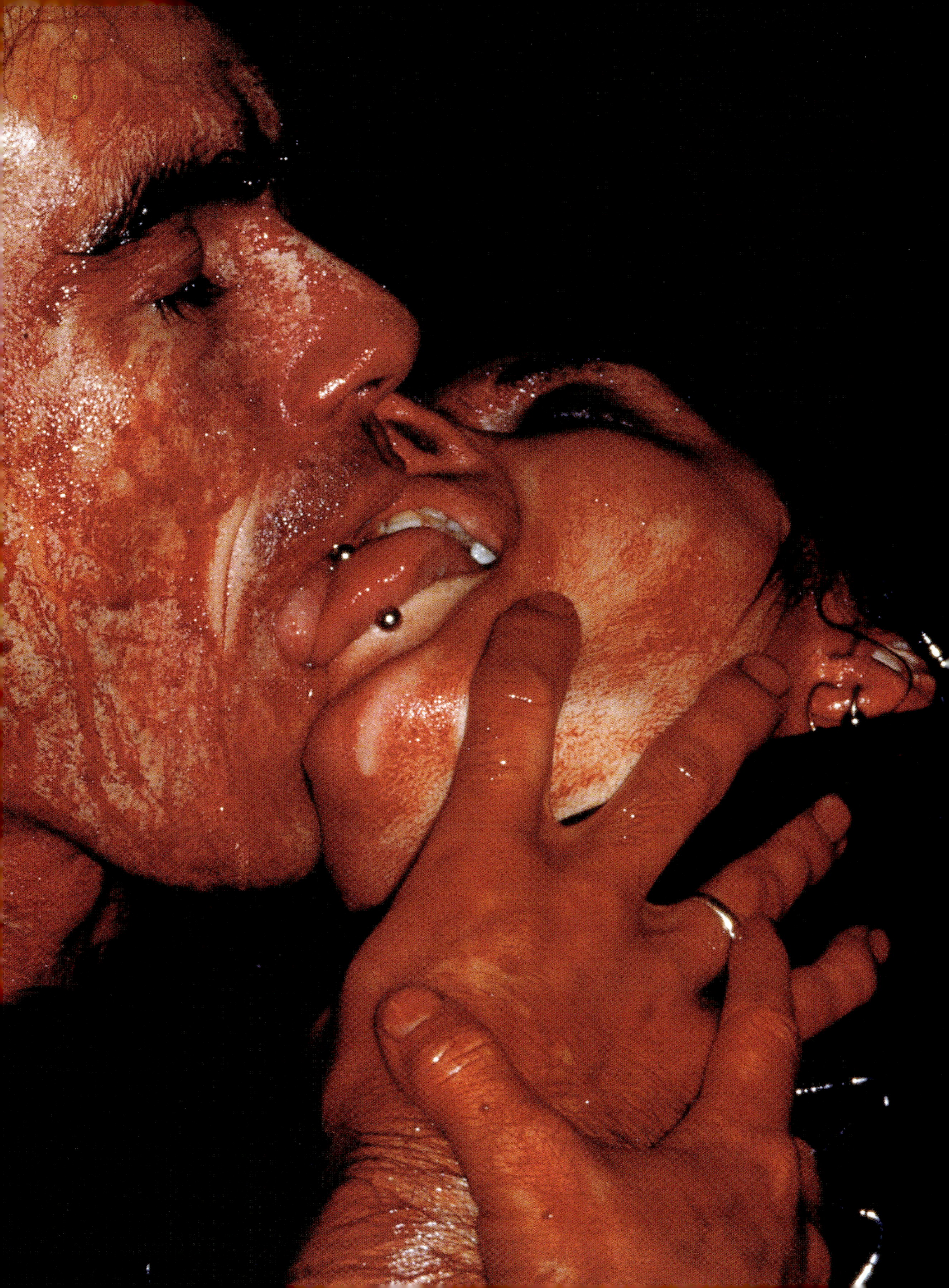

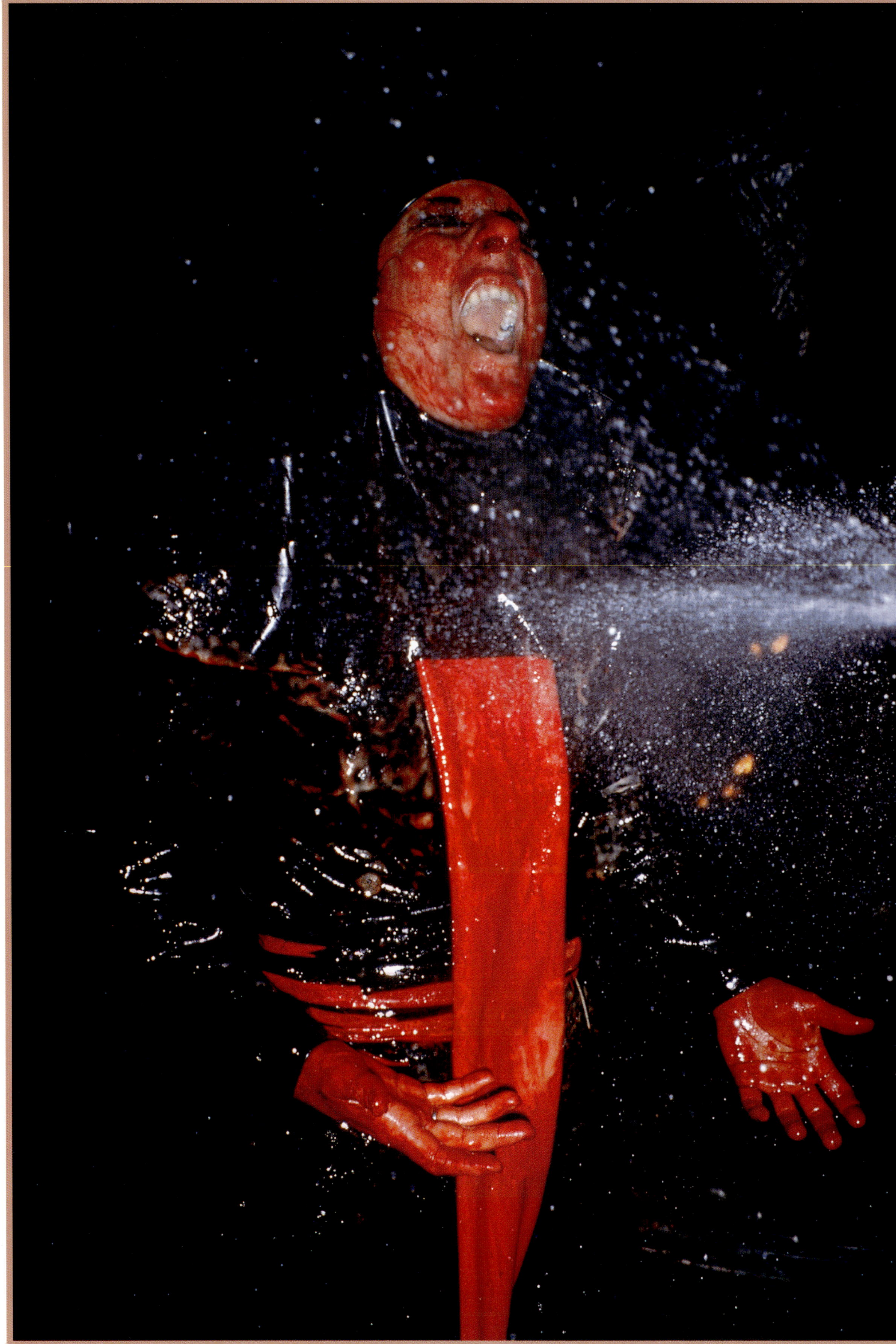

in order of appearance

Dharma
Danielle Willis
Clint Catalyst
Jennifer Pieren
falcon
Dragon
Mistress Zea
Gabriele
the Rev. Steven Johnson Leyba
Jobbe Eagle
Mistress Taira
Violet Hemlock
Elizabeth Berrian
Hannah
Louis Bonz
Onya Bonz
Todd Ruin
Michael Decker
Lily Burana

Blood wedding sequence shot at Burning Man Festival, Black Rock Desert, Nevada, September 1996.
Apache Whiskey Ritual shot at USAF performance, 848 Divisadero, San Francisco, Halloween 1996.
Dragon and Zea's ritual shot at Hanger 18, March 1995.

afterword.

Blood cults, blood rituals, blood healing practices and vampirism have been with us consistently and cross-culturally since the dawn of recorded history.

If any trends are discernible, one would note the replacement of blood healing practices by modern medicine, and the remarkable differentiation of vampirism.

The mythic and folkloric vampire, resting on a foundation of widespread human experience, was supplemented by the literary vampire {see Coleridge (1816), Lord Byron (1817), Shelley (1818), Polidori (1819), Keats (1820), Gautier (1836), LeFanu (1872), and, of course, Stoker (1897)}, who immediately mutated, yielding the vampires of stage, opera and screen.

Most recently, this impressively adaptable species can be found in cyberspace. On the Internet, you can enter vampire chat rooms, and Web pages numbering in the thousands bring you pertinent books, organizations, conferences, fan clubs, and rather elaborate live-action role-playing games.

Whether symbol (of life, birth, regeneration, bonding, commitment, pain and expurgation) or substance, blood fascinates well beyond its special appeal to the vampire. It can be as meaningful to the girl next door on her wedding day as it is to the mystic who employs self-flagellation to draw blood to facilitate an altered state of consciousness.

As a psychologist it is my privilege to guide people as they descend into and return from their private hells. If one wants to get to heaven, one must first visit hell, as Dante so ably demonstrated. Hell is populated by our demons – devils in need of transformation.

> *The more devils we have within us, the more chance we have to form angels.*
> *"Angel" is the name we give to repentant devils – so have faith.*
> Nikos Kazantzakis

Here we encounter one of the more difficult of life's paradoxes: to transform our devils, we must not oppose them, for whenever we try to silence them with moral indignation, they submerge, only to become more formidable, more hideous.

However, non-judgmental acceptance (which is neither disapproval nor approval but detached neutrality) must not be confused with indulgence.

The line is often as thin as a razor's edge. Rule of thumb: as we dance with our demons, the more freely chosen the dance, the more transformative; but the more compulsive the dance, however revelatory of the trauma which fuels it, the more it tends to preserve unconsciousness. (Rule not subject to scientific verification.)

It cannot be said, without interviewing the subjects of this book, whether they are choosing or are compelled to dance. Some dances, initially chosen, can become relentlessly compelling. Some dances, even if volitional, may harbor unanticipated dangers for both body and psyche. Dance at your own risk.

Above all, if and when we dance with our demons, we must honor and respect them. The dance is sacred and also very private. Seldom does anyone allow another to behold it.

Yet, a fair witness is essential to the transformation of devil into angel. The witness, too, must honor and respect both dancer and dance, must hear with understanding.

> *Hermes: "The hearer... should think with him who speaks and breath with him; nay, he should have a hearing subtler than the voice of him who speaks."*
> *Corpus Hermeticum X:17*

The Witness completes the triangle: dancer, demon and witness are one in the dance. Beyond space-time. How many minutes or years one must dance with a particular demon cannot be said.

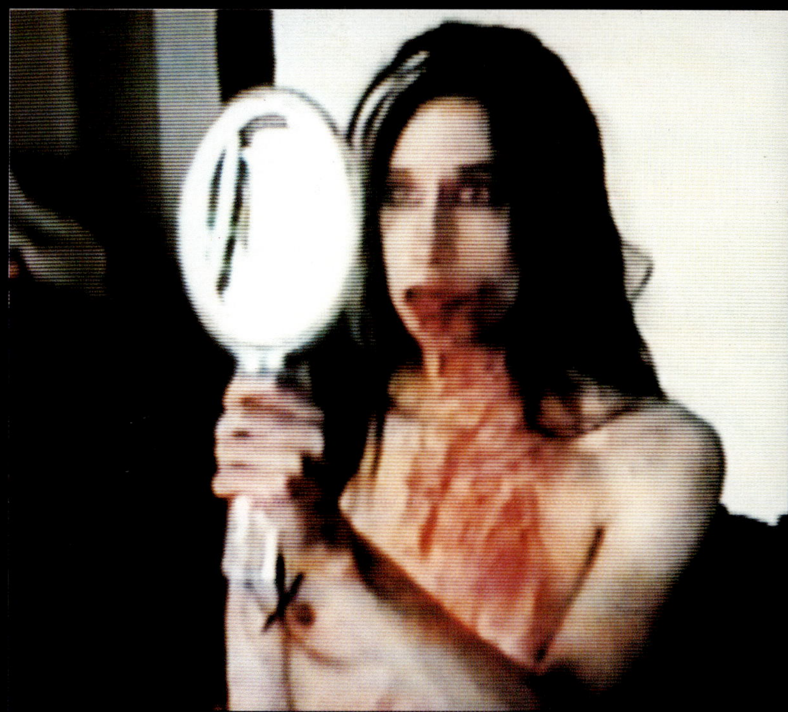

Few artists have recorded this dance without distortion. Saint Augustine, Saint Teresa of Avila, Dante, Dostoyevsky, Kafka, Bach, Verdi, Tchaikovsky, Bosch, Delacroix. Now a photographer and prose-poet join the ranks.

Had an anthropologist brought these images from another continent, another century, they might be less evocative. If, instead of consenting adults, Charles Gatewood had photographed the estimated 650 virginal victims of Countess Elizabeth Bathory (1560-1614), they again might be less evocative, for there is some comfort in unambivalent condemnation. But Danielle Willis is the proverbial girl next door.

With his quiet, unintrusive steadiness, Gatewood, anthropologist at heart, comes to witness and record. He has not come to judge, and his subjects know it. In the openings he creates, dancers and demons embrace, and souls are revealed.

David Aaron Clark, himself familiar with the lure and taste of human blood, uses language to bridge from dancer dancing to the image of the dance to the conscious and unconscious mind of the beholder – a bridge on which we may travel as far and as long as our honesty and understanding will support us. But Clark, who moves fluidly in and out of role, does not insist that his is the only bridge. You are free to create your own – or burn it.

Blood: a symbol. Blood: a corporeal reality. Indelible. For better or for worse.

Daniel Lapin. Ph.D.
San Francisco. California

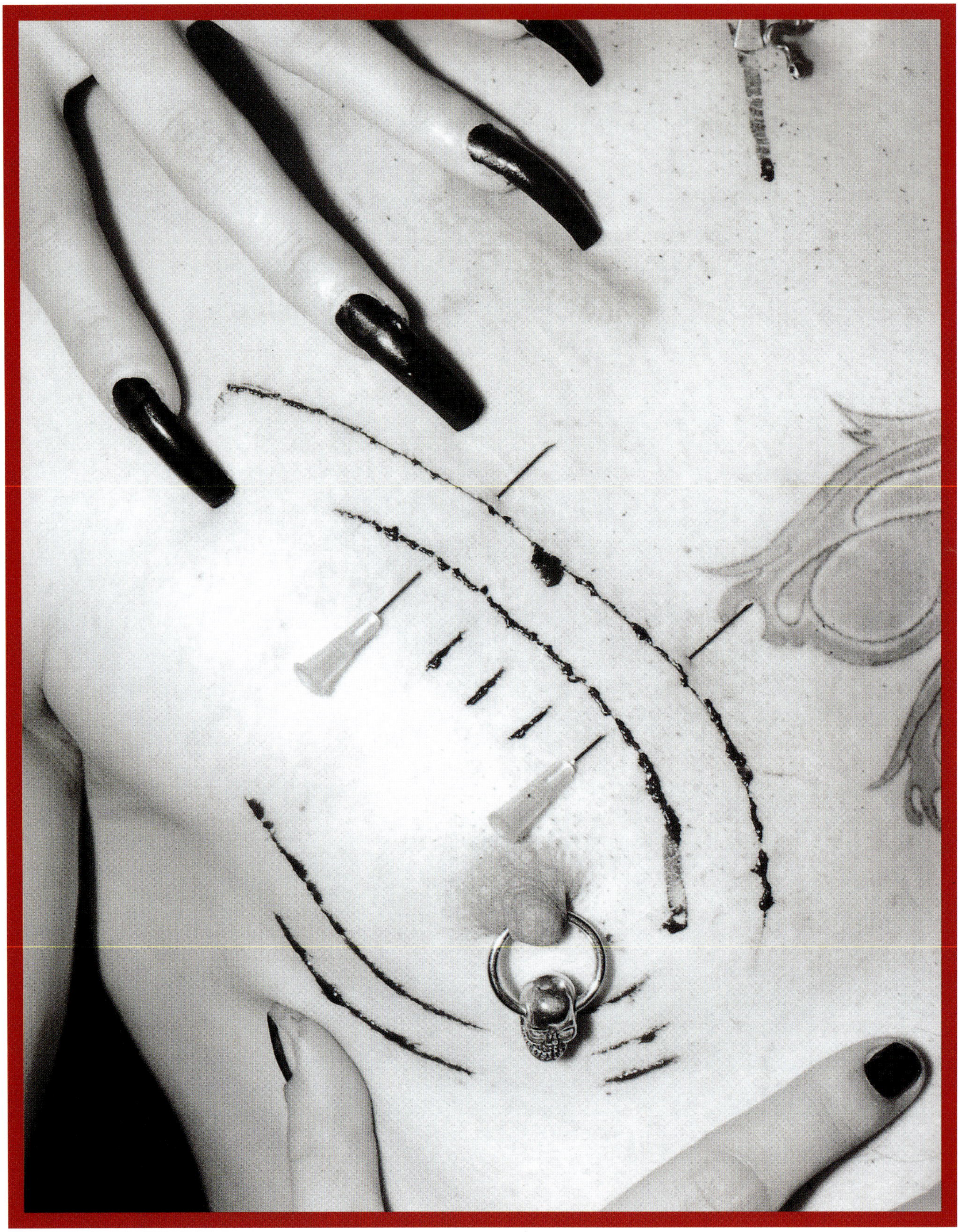

Charles Gatewood's striking photographs have been exhibited and published to international acclaim. Gatewood's books include *Sidetripping* (with William S. Burroughs), *Wall Street, Forbidden Photographs, Pushing Ink* (with Spider Webb), *Charles Gatewood Photographs: The Body and Beyond,* and *Primitives*. His photography has been supported by three fellowships from the New York State Council on the Arts, and by numerous awards, including the Leica Medal of Excellence for Outstanding Humanistic Photojournalism.

David Aaron Clark is a journalist, fiction writer, musician and performer. His novels include *The Wet Forever, Sister Radiance, Juliette: Vengeance on the Lord* and *Into the Black*. He also co-edited the anthology *Ritual Sex* with Tristan Taormino. His own blood-sex performances are recorded on the video *Bleeding Heart,* and with his band False Virgins he has recorded two albums, *Skinjob* and *Infernal Doll.* His journalism career includes stints with both Dow Jones News Service and *Screw* magazine.

Daniel Lapin, Ph.D. is a licensed psychologist with 22 years of clinical experience. He received his B.S. and M.S. from Cornell University, and received the Ph.D. in psychology from the California Institute of Integral Studies in San Francisco. He is the author of *The Vampire, Dracula and Incest: The Vampire Myth, Stoker's* Dracula *and Psychotherapy of Vampiric Sexual Abuse*. He is in private practice in San Francisco.

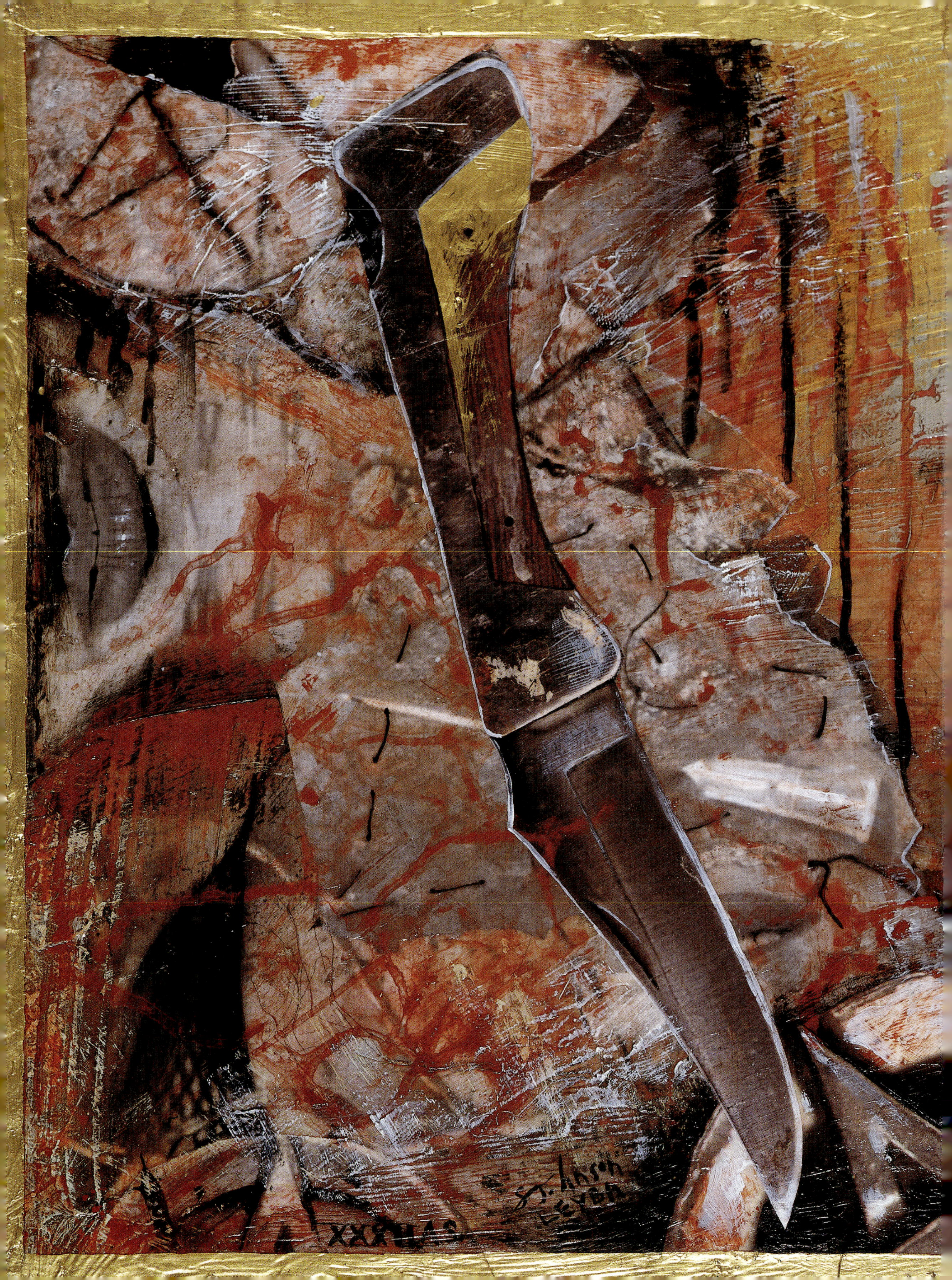